PURRFECT KIBBLE

THE MYSTERIES OF MAX 82

NIC SAINT

PURRFECT KIBBLE

The Mysteries of Max 82

Copyright © 2024 by Nic Saint

All rights reserved. No part of this book may be reproduced in any form by any electronic or mechanical means including photocopying, recording, or information storage and retrieval without permission in writing from the author.

This is a work of fiction. Names, characters, places, brands, media, and incidents are either the product of the author's imagination or are used fictitiously. The author acknowledges the trademarked status and trademark owners of various products referenced in this work of fiction, which have been used without permission. The publication/use of these trademarks is not authorized, associated with, or sponsored by the trademark owners.

Edited by Chereese Graves

www.nicsaint.com

Give feedback on the book at: info@nicsaint.com

facebook.com/nicsaintauthor
@nicsaintauthor

First Edition

Printed in the U.S.A

PURRFECT KIBBLE

Caddicts of the World, Unite!

It had been one of those unseasonably hot days that makes me want to dig a hole in the ground and disappear when Dooley discovered treasure in the pantry: three bags of original Franklin Cooper kibble. The factory had gone bust three years ago, so this could very well be the last of the legendary kibble maker's delicious goodies. Unfortunately for us, we weren't the only ones who were after the treat. Odelia wanted to dump it in the trash, ants wanted to steal it and a gang of drug dealers had designs on it for their own nefarious reasons. Along the way we were faced with murder, mayhem and even a car chase. But in spite of all this, we were steadfast in our goal of preserving the Franklin Cooper legacy.

CHAPTER 1

Dooley had been rooting around in the pantry when his nostrils suddenly were filled with a familiar scent. It smelled very much like… kibble! And not just any type of kibble but his favorite kind. The one Odelia used to buy but for some reason that he couldn't fathom had stopped getting for them. And here, buried underneath a pile of old clothes that were destined to be thrown out, several bags had been hiding all along! For a moment, he struggled to contain the powerful emotion this momentous discovery elicited. But then only one thought stood out: he had to tell someone. And not just someone. He had to tell Max. And so he quickly tiptoed out of the pantry, hoping Odelia hadn't noticed his snooping around, and went in search of his friend. He found him stretched out on the lawn, lying spread-eagle as was his latest habit, in a bid to cool his voluminous body by soaking up the coolness of the lawn. Those grass blades had their work cut out for them!

"Max!" he whispered as he lay down next to his friend. "Max, I just made the most amazing discovery!"

"You found a fan?" asked Max, who didn't like the heat

and was suffering something terrible every time the sun decided to turn the world below into a furnace. "Or did Chase finally get us that portable air conditioner he's been promising he would buy?"

"None of the above," he said. "I found Franklin Cooper kibble." For a moment, Max didn't respond, and he wondered if his friend hadn't heard him. "I said I found—"

"I heard you," Max said. Then he looked up at Dooley with a wild surmise. "You actually found Franklin Cooper kibble? But I thought the business went belly-up? At least that's what I heard."

"I didn't know that," Dooley admitted. It saddened him to know that Franklin Cooper had gone out of business. "I found three whole bags in the pantry, hidden underneath a pile of old clothes. I had a quick sniff, and they smell just fine. In fact, they smell as glorious as I remember."

A beatific look had stolen over the large blorange cat's face. "I remember that smell. They were the best kibble we'd ever tasted in our lives, weren't they?"

"They sure were," said Dooley. "And now we can taste them again. But we have to be smart about this, Max. I don't know why Odelia decided to hide them from us—or maybe she simply forgot she still had them. But I have a feeling that when she finds out that we found out, they'll disappear. Just a hunch."

"You're absolutely right, Dooley," said Max. Then he frowned. "Have you told anyone else about this?"

"I have not," he assured his best companion.

"Brutus?" he asked, referring to their housemate.

He shook his head. "The moment I found them, I came straight here to tell you about it, since I figured you'd know what to do."

"I think you made a wise decision not to let Odelia know that you have discovered that kibble," said Max. For a moment, he thought deeply, exercising that large brain of his, then finally he nodded. "I think it's probably safe to assume that Odelia simply forgot that she still had them. Which means..."

Dooley's face lit up with a look of excitement. "Which means..."

"Which means that we may very well be in possession of the very last bags of Franklin Cooper kibble available anywhere on the planet!"

Dooley's face sagged. "But that also means..."

"It also means we probably shouldn't eat it," said Max as his face displayed the same sense of disappointment. "Which is exactly why those bags will go missing again the moment Odelia finds out. She doesn't like to offer us food whose expiration date has elapsed."

"I won't tell her if you won't," Dooley suggested. Then another thought struck him. "But if these bags are the last Franklin Cooper bags on the planet, that means they're extremely rare, Max."

His friend nodded seriously. "Exactly. That kibble has become a rare commodity, Dooley. In fact it isn't too much to say it's probably priceless by now. Some people might even want to put it in a museum or maybe a wealthy collector might be willing to pay a ginormous price for these very same bags."

"Like a Van Gogh, you mean?" asked Dooley.

"Exactly like a Van Gogh," said Max. "After an artist dies, you know the price of their work suddenly increases exponentially. So the same might be true for the Franklin Cooper kibble."

"Do you think Franklin Cooper died, and that's why he stopped making his very fine kibble?"

"I think that's a safe assumption," said Max. "Franklin Cooper died, and since he was possibly the best pet food maker in the history of the world—a real master in the art of pet food making: one of those rare geniuses that only come around every couple of generations—we should honor him and not eat his kibble but save it for posterity."

"Maybe others can study his kibble and discover his secret recipe?" Dooley suggested.

"That may very well be true," Max agreed. "Reverse-engineering is a thing, Dooley."

Just then, Harriet and Brutus came toddling up. They, too, looked a little overheated and could have used a cool environment to rest their weary heads. The moment they joined them, the conversation halted, and Dooley exchanged a knowing glance with his friend. 'We'll talk about this later,' Dooley's glance said. 'Once the coast is clear,' was Max's non-verbal response. Franklin Cooper kibble was a topic too sensitive and important to become the subject of idle speculation and conversation.

* * *

"Are you guys also hot?" asked Harriet. "My brain is melting."

"My brain is also melting," said Brutus. He glanced over to Max. "You look extremely hot, Max. But then that's probably to be expected as you've got possibly the largest brain of any cat I know."

"How do you combat the heat?" asked Harriet.

"Well, I lay on the grass, for one thing," said Max. "In the shade, of course. And I've asked Dooley to go look for that old fan that Odelia once bought. Remember that fan?"

"Oh, do I remember that fan?" said Harriet fervently as a yearning look came into her eyes. "We used to lie in front of that fan, remember? The only thing that possibly provided some coolness on a hot day like today."

"And did you find it?" asked Brutus.

"I didn't," said Dooley. "I looked for it everywhere but couldn't find it."

"Maybe Odelia got rid of it," said Brutus. "Or maybe it broke. These things always break down, you know." He remembered from the olden days when he still lived with Chase's mom and aunt in New York that their fans would always break down through some faulty design or disabuse at the hands of his humans. Couldn't they understand that pets suffered even more from the heat than humans did? Then he got a bright idea. "Maybe we should go and spend a couple of hours in the basement. It's mostly cooler there."

"There's probably mice in the basement," said Harriet. "Or worse: rats!"

"I don't care," said Brutus valiantly. "As long as it's cool, I don't mind at all."

And so it was decided. In the absence of their human to locate that fan, or even buy them a new one, they'd temporarily relocate to the basement and wait until this crazy day was over. Then when night had fallen, they could emerge and enjoy the coolness of the night.

"I envy humans," said Harriet as they made their way through the pet flap and into the house. "When it's hot like this, they simply take a cold shower, or a cold bath, or use that paddling pool that Chase hauled out for Grace."

She was right, Brutus thought. Humans were to be envied for their appreciation of the cold splash on their faces or the capacity to be submerged in a body of cooling water and have no qualms about it whatsoever. If they submerged him in a paddling pool, he'd scream bloody murder and not show his face around the premises for days—until the danger had passed. As it was, Grace had gotten into the habit of splashing water all over them, whether by design or by accident. He didn't like it, and so they had vowed not to come anywhere near the little girl if they could help it. Not as long as this heatwave persisted and Grace spent most of her leisure time splashing around in her little plastic pool.

And as they descended into the basement, taking those stone steps that led into the underbelly of the house, he could feel the temperature drop to a more tolerable degree. And as they hunkered down on the concrete floor, his body relaxed. He hadn't known how stressful this heat could be on his corporeal being. And he wasn't even the most hefty specimen in their troupe, with Max tipping the scales much higher. He couldn't imagine how much the big cat must be suffering right now. And as they inspected their new hidey-hole, he didn't think there were any mice on the premises. Not like before, when an entire colony took up position down there and treated it as their own home.

"No mice," he reassured his mate. "And no rats either."

There were a few bugs, and some spiders dangling from their webs in the corners of the ceiling, but that couldn't be helped. And anyway, they posed no threat to them whatsoever. He stretched himself out on the concrete floor and closed his eyes with relish. The concrete was cool on his tummy and exactly what he needed right now.

"I love it," he murmured happily. "I love it so much."

"Yeah, it's pretty good down here," Harriet agreed. "Though a little dark, wouldn't you say? Not to mention not very cozy."

"I don't care," he said as he seemed to melt into the floor. "I don't care at all." Who needs cozy when your body is about to expire from the heat?

For a moment, none of them spoke as the four cats made themselves comfortable and vowed to stay there until the weather turned. Then suddenly Dooley piped up, "I'm sorry, Max, but I can't stay quiet."

"Dooley!" said Max. "No!"

"Harriet and Brutus are our friends, Max!"

"But you promised!"

"I'm sorry, but I can't keep quiet any longer."

"What's going on?" asked Brutus, curious about this sudden outburst.

Dooley still seemed to be struggling with himself, and as he locked eyes with Max, finally the latter sighed. "Okay, fine. I guess it's not very nice to keep this momentous discovery to ourselves. Not to mention selfish." And so he directed a serious look at Brutus. "Dooley was looking for that fan."

"And he didn't find it, right?" said Harriet. "If only he had, then we wouldn't have to spend time down here, in this dank old cellar." She made a face. "I'm sure this floor hasn't been washed in years. It's dirty, you guys, and I can feel its grime staining my precious fur. Now I'll have to groom myself and get all of that dirt into my—"

"I found three bags of Franklin Cooper kibble!" suddenly Dooley blurted.

For a moment, none of them spoke, then Brutus overcame his surprise and said, "You found three bags of the best kibble in the world?"

Dooley nodded fervently. "Only now we don't know what to do with it. Maybe we could sell it to the highest bidder, like a Van Gogh painting. Or we could send it to the lab and have it reverse-engineered so they can make more of it. Or we could simply eat it. What do you think?"

Brutus gave Max a look of surprise, and when he saw the expression of guilt on the big cat's face, he thought he saw it all. "You weren't going to tell us, were you? You were going to keep this a secret and eat that delicious kibble all by yourself!"

"I wasn't going to eat it!" said Max defensively. "I was going to figure out what to do about those bags. Like Dooley said, those may very well be the last bags of Franklin Cooper kibble in the whole wide world, and so we have a responsibility to make the right choice."

His blorange friend had a point. If these were indeed the final remaining bags of Franklin Cooper, they couldn't simply eat it. That would border on sacrilege. "I like the idea of taking them to the lab and having them cloned," he said. "That way we could create as much of that kibble as we like." The thought of snacking on that most delicious and nutritious kibble made his mouth water and his eyes glaze over. As they hadn't had any of the stuff for years, it had taken on an almost mythical reputation in cat circles. Even Kingman, whose owner Wilbur Vickery mostly got him the best kibble that money could buy, hadn't been able to lay his hands on real Franklin Cooper kibble in many years.

"Or we could sell it," he suggested. "I'll bet there are people willing to pay through the nose for the last bags of Franklin Cooper. I'm talking hundreds, maybe even thousands of dollars per bag."

"It is a collector's item," Harriet agreed. "Though considering it's also a perishable product, maybe it won't fetch as much as you think, sugar cookie."

"And I think it will. People keep old chocolate bars from fifty years ago if it contains some football card or something. True collectors are weird in that sense, you know. Or they'll keep some old Coca-Cola can if it was a special edition," he added. "Even though that soda must have turned by now."

Harriet made a face. "Imagine having to drink that."

"That's the whole point," said Brutus. "They'll never drink it. Just put it in a glass display case and stare at it from time to time and show it off to other collectors."

Looks like they were faced with a very important decision that had possible ramifications far beyond the simple fact that they were the proud owners of a unique and rare type of kibble.

And as the four of them gave themselves up to thought, all of a sudden a small voice sounded right next to him. "Are you guys planning on staying long?"

He looked in the direction of the voice and saw a small black ant staring up at him, its antennae moving anxiously. Then as he glanced beyond the ant, he saw a conga line of thousands more ants, all waiting to move along. Looked like he was lying right on top of a busy ant highway!

CHAPTER 2

I watched the progress, or rather the lack of progress, of that column of ants with a doleful eye. It has been said that when you get ants in the home, the homeowner despairs, and even though I'm not the actual owner of the home I have graced with my presence all of these past years, I still feel a sense of ownership about the place, exactly because of my long association with the premises. It might not be too much to say I feel a sense of fondness. And so to see an army of ants traipsing about the place filled me with a sensation of dread.

Brutus must have felt the same way, for as he slowly got up to allow those ants free passage, he did so more out of fear that they would walk all over him than out of some notion that he should let these ants pass.

"Do you guys live here?" he asked.

"Where are you going?" asked Dooley.

"Have you been here long?" asked Harriet with a look of horror on her fine features.

"Shouldn't you be out there instead of down here?" I asked, clearly showing my negative bias.

The leader of the ants—or at least the one leading the troop—now turned to us, and I could see its antennae twitch in response to our barrage of questions. "Okay, one question at a time," he said. "Yes, home, yes and no. Does that answer all of your questions?"

"Well, no," I said. "I mean, do you have permission to be here, Mr..."

"Lucian," he said. "The name is Lucian. And you are?"

"Max," I said. "And these are my friends Dooley, Harriet, and Brutus."

"That's fine," said Lucian, and traipsed on in the direction of the corner of the room. And as we watched, his army of ants approached the wall, but instead of disappearing into a hole or crevice, they simply started walking up the wall. It's not something that cats are capable of doing, for obvious reasons: our paws don't have that stickiness that allows us to walk on walls and ceilings and defy gravity in that way.

"Um... could you tell us where you are going?" I asked. The answer he had given us wasn't entirely to my satisfaction. Home? But this was our home. He couldn't possibly mean that he was going to infest it with the presence of his entire flock? Or is it a gathering? Or maybe even a collection?

"Like I said, we're going home," said the ant in charge of this particular troop.

"And where is home for you, Lucian?" asked Harriet, overcoming her aversion and trying to engage the ant leader in conversation.

"Up there," said Lucian, and gestured with his tiny head in the direction of the ceiling, which was fast approaching for him and his followers.

"But... you're not actually going to live in our living room, are you?" asked Brutus. "I mean, that wouldn't be very nice of you."

"And I'm sure Odelia and Chase wouldn't appreciate it if an army of ants moved into their living room," I said.

"It's a colony," said Lucian coldly.

"Pardon me?" I said.

"I prefer the word colony over army," he explained. The army—or colony—had almost reached the ceiling—they were pretty fast, I had to admit—and as we watched on, suddenly Lucian simply disappeared into a tiny crack in the ceiling and was gone, to be followed in short order by the other members of his flock.

"I don't like this, Max," said Dooley. "They're going to eat all of our Franklin Cooper kibble!"

And as I gave him a startled look, I remembered that the pantry where he had made this wonderful discovery was located directly above us!

"Oh, no," said Brutus. "Don't tell me the Franklin Cooper is in the pantry?"

Dooley nodded sadly.

"But that means…"

He nodded again.

"We have to save that kibble, you guys," said Harriet. "We can't allow an army—"

"Or colony," I ventured.

"Whatever—to eat the last remaining Franklin Cooper on the planet. It won't do!"

She was right, and so in spite of the fact that we had vowed not to leave that basement until the weather turned, we hurried back up those stone steps and made our way into the pantry where Dooley had made his startling discovery. The odd thing was that of the ants, there wasn't a single trace. It was almost as if they had simply disappeared.

"Where are they?" asked Brutus, rooting around the pantry in search of these tiny creatures.

"No idea," I said, but the sense of relief I felt was certainly palpable, I have to say.

"Where is that kibble, Dooley?" asked Harriet, wasting no time to get down to business.

Our friend showed us the location of the Franklin Cooper, and much to our relief, the bags hadn't been compromised. The seals were still closed, and it was obvious that the kibble was still as it had been on the day that Odelia had made the purchase.

"Those ants will not be able to get through this plastic, will they?" asked Brutus as he gave the bags a loving nudge with the top of his head.

"Of course they can bite their way through that plastic," I said, finding myself forced to rain on my friend's parade. "They can probably chew through anything."

"Not concrete, though, right?" said Dooley. "Right?"

I didn't have an answer for him, but it was my distinct impression that ants can also chew their way through stone and concrete and the like, which didn't bode well for our future.

It was at that moment that the door to the pantry opened, and Odelia walked in. As she turned on the light, she was startled to find four cats looking up at her. And as her eyes traveled to the bags of Franklin Cooper, we knew that our secret was out.

"Oh, my God!" she said, bringing a hand to her face. "I'd totally forgotten about those. Where did you find them?"

"They were hidden underneath a pile of old clothes," Dooley said. "Odelia, are these the last remaining Franklin Cooper bags on the face of the earth?"

"If that's the case, we should preserve them for posterity," said Harriet.

"And send them to the lab to have the recipe reverse-engineered," I added.

Odelia laughed. "I'm sure there must be more Franklin Cooper bags in the world apart from these. It's just that I'd totally forgotten I got these. I've actually been looking for them."

She clearly hadn't looked very good, or otherwise she would have found them. But since I was in a mellow sort of mood, owing to the fact that I was entirely too hot, I was prepared to forgive her for this oversight, which is why it pained me to have to break the bad news to her.

"We have ants," I said. "An entire army of them."

"Or colony," Brutus corrected me.

"We have ants?" asked Odelia, and the way she said it gave me the impression that she wasn't a big fan of the species either. "Where are they?"

"Well, they were in the basement just now," said Brutus. "And they came straight up here, but for some reason they've gone missing, so we have no idea where they are now."

"A lot of ants?" she said in a strangled sort of voice as she bit her lip.

The four of us nodded seriously. "An entire army," said Brutus.

"Or colony," I muttered.

"Maybe you should put those bags in a different place," Harriet suggested. "Just in case they are the last remaining bags of Franklin Cooper on the planet, we don't want those ants to get at them, do we?"

"Maybe that's why we have them," said Odelia. "Food attracts ants, after all." She glanced around, and when she didn't see any other source of nourishment, she picked up the three bags and took them from the pantry. And since I felt very much attached to those bags, I tripped after her and so did my three friends.

"Are you going to send them to the lab to have them reverse-engineered?" I asked.

"Or to Sotheby's to have them auctioned off to the highest bidder?" asked Brutus.

"Or saved for posterity?" asked Dooley.

"Or maybe we can have a nibble now," I suggested. "Just to make sure they're still fine?"

"I will do nothing of the kind," said Odelia. "You can have a nibble when your other kibble is finished. Opened bags lose their freshness, as you well know." And she opened one of the kitchen cupboards and stored the bags in there, where we couldn't get at them, and hopefully the ants couldn't either. I could have told her this was wishful thinking, since ants can walk on walls, on the ceiling, and most certainly can get into any storage space without batting an eyelid—if they have eyelids, that is. I may be thinking of a different kind of bug.

"She's going to feed it to us, Max," said Dooley, his voice hushed in awe. "She's going to feed us actual Franklin Cooper kibble!"

"Too bad," said Harriet. "If this really is the last remaining Franklin Cooper on the planet, we shouldn't eat it, you guys. It's sacrilege. And I, for one, wouldn't feel easy in my mind if we simply ate it all—no matter how good it is," she hastened to add when Brutus opened his mouth to protest such a narrow-minded point of view.

Though I had to agree there was probably something in what she said. Would you drink the last bottle of Coca-Cola on the planet? Or eat the last Big Mac? Or would you save it for posterity? Or to put in a museum? To be honest, I had to admit that a battle raged inside of my bosom. On the one paw, I couldn't wait to dig my teeth into that delicious kibble and enjoy that great taste. On the other paw, we had to think of the future—a future without Franklin Cooper wasn't much of a future, now was it?

And so we all decided that a decision needed to be made

on this—a decision that wasn't borne of our own selfish needs but had the wellbeing of the entire global community of cats at heart. A heavy responsibility had been placed on our narrow shoulders, but we wouldn't be the cats that we were if we weren't prepared to face it head-on.

CHAPTER 3

Dooley had been thinking hard about what to do about the predicament they faced. In his young life, he had never been disobedient to Odelia, but now, for the first time, he wondered if maybe he shouldn't follow his instincts instead of his sense of loyalty to their human. If asked, he would have said that the ants had caused this rupture in his mindset. If they reached that prime kibble and set about to devour it and feed it to their colony, that would be the end of the Franklin Cooper legacy—that fine, fine kibble maker. Perhaps the finest one that had ever lived. And then where would they be? They couldn't allow that to happen. Much like the vandals that had ransacked Rome, these ants simply had to be stopped. And since it's very hard to stop an army of ants—or even a colony—once it gets going, the only solution he saw was to make sure their prize was gone. In other words: no loot - no thief.

He had vowed to take this important matter up with Max, but much to his surprise, Max didn't seem all that worried about the dilemma they faced. When he looked, he actually saw that his friend had mysteriously disappeared and was nowhere to be found. Dooley looked everywhere: upstairs, in the backyard, even next door, but the end result was the same: no Max!

Finally, it dawned on him that his friend was the one suffering the most from this heatwave they were experiencing and had perhaps simply returned to the safe haven of the basement, the only place in the house where it was more or less reasonably cool. And so he hurried down the stairs once more to locate his friend. He found him stretched out on the concrete floor looking miserable.

"Max, what's wrong!" he asked as he joined the large cat.

"Too... hot..." Max groaned without opening his eyes.

"I know, I know," he said soothingly. "Maybe I could ask Odelia to buy another fan and to put it down here?"

Max nodded. "That would be nice," he sighed desperately.

And so Dooley went in search of their human and found her in the kitchen engaged in dinner prep. "Odelia, could you possibly buy a fan?" he asked. "Max is expiring," he explained. "He can't stand this terrible heat."

"I'm sorry to hear that, Dooley," said Odelia absentmindedly. "Where is he?"

"In the basement," he said. "Trying to lower his body temperature but failing."

"I thought we had one," said Odelia. "Did you look in the storeroom?"

"I did, and it's nowhere to be found," he said, appreciating her helpful approach.

"I'll ask Chase to pick one up on his way home from work," she said as she grabbed something from the cupboard. As she did, she accidentally must have struck her hand against one of the bags of kibble she had stored there, for it fell down from there and dropped on the floor. As it did, the bag burst, and a small avalanche of kibble spread across the kitchen floor.

"Noooooooo!!!!!" Dooley cried as he watched all of that precious kibble going to waste.

"Oh, God," Odelia muttered as she bent down to pick up the bag. Horrified, Dooley watched as she grabbed a duster and dustpan and proceeded to scoop up the spilled kibble… and dump it in the trash!

"Odelia, what are you doing!" he yelled.

"It's spoiled," she explained.

"It's Franklin Cooper!"

"You can't expect me to give this kibble to you after it's been on the floor," she said as she deposited it into the trash can and closed the lid with a decisive gesture.

"Is there at least something left in the bag?" he asked with a pained heart.

"Some," she said as she rattled the bag. Judging from the sound, there wasn't a whole lot left in there, most of it having ended up in the trash.

This was simply terrible—such a waste!

He glanced up at the cupboard and saw that there were only two bags left now. If those also dropped to the floor, gone would be Franklin Cooper's rare and precious gift to the world.

Which is when he decided that in spite of his reservations, his plan had to be carried out. And the only one smart enough to think up a way to accomplish it was Max. Now if only they could cool down his brain enough to return it to working order…

* * *

I HAVE to say that being in a position where your body heat is elevated isn't a nice one to be in. Oddly enough, it seemed to affect my mental capacity mostly, but also my general mood, which was lethargic and downcast, as if the weight of the world was bearing down on me. I didn't like to feel this way, and sincerely hoped it wouldn't be long before things returned to normal. And so when Dooley came hurrying down the stairs again and told me that our favorite kibble was in danger of going extinct, it certainly didn't help matters. What it did do was instill in me a desire to live through this terrible ordeal and turn things around.

"We have to save our kibble," said Dooley. "Before Odelia puts it all in the trash."

"You're right," I muttered. Even though the concrete floor I had picked as my new favorite place was a little cooler than the rest of the house, it wasn't exactly cool enough to my liking.

"Chase is going to buy a fan," my friend told me as he gave me a look of concern.

"Good."

"It'll help cool you off."

"Thanks, Dooley." I had closed my eyes for a moment, but I could sense that he was looking at me intently, so I opened them again. "What is it?"

"We need to come up with a plan. And when I say 'we,' I mean 'you.' So what can we do to save our kibble, Max? We need to act fast, you see. The callousness with which Odelia treats our kibble doesn't bode well for the future. Add to that the ant menace, and something needs to be done."

"Ask Harriet," I said feebly. Clearly, she wasn't suffering from the heat as much as I was, and she had a vested interest in making sure that the kibble was saved from destruction.

"'Ask Harriet,'" he repeated, making a mental note. "Good plan. Excellent plan." He gave me an uncertain look. "But do you think it'll be enough? We both know Harriet is a lot of things but she's not exactly a mastermind."

"Ask Brutus," I tried.

"I will," he said, nodding. "I'll ask Harriet and Brutus. But even though Brutus is a real action cat, he's not, shall we say, the smartest cat on the block. That's you, Max. And right now, what we need is not brawn but brain, if you see what I mean."

"Ask… Fifi," I finally managed with what felt like my final breath. "She's… smart."

If he said anything else, I didn't catch it, for my brain pretty much shut down after that. One can only take so much, and even though I wanted to help in any way I could, my body, for reasons entirely of its own, decided otherwise.

CHAPTER 4

'Ask Harriet,' Dooley thought. 'Ask Brutus. Ask Fifi.' He cheered up considerably. Of all the pets they knew, Fifi was quite possibly the smartest one. There was also Rufus, of course, their neighbors' sheepdog, but he was just a lovable big floofball. Not exactly a major threat in the brain department. And so as he mounted the stairs back to the ground floor and hurried out of the house through the pet flap, he decided to follow Max's advice—possibly the final advice the big cat would give before expiring and moving to the feline Valhalla—and went in search of Fifi, their neighbor Kurt Mayfield's Yorkshire Terrier.

He found the doggie in the backyard of her home, half submerged in a small paddling pool her owner had installed for her there. It wasn't in the same league as the paddling pool Chase had installed for Grace, but it was definitely a thing of beauty. And most importantly, it was filled with cool water. Dogs may be a lot of things, but they're not afraid of water, that much was evidenced by the sight that met his eyes.

"You're not suffering from the heat, are you?" he asked.

"No, not really," said Fifi. "This paddling pool is absolutely great." She gestured to the spot next to her. "Dive in, Dooley. The water is great."

He respectfully declined. He might be suffering from the heat to some extent, but his aversion to getting wet was even stronger than the tortures he was facing. "I have a very important mission for you, Fifi," he said. "It may very well be the most important mission of your life."

"A matter of life or death, huh?" said Fifi.

"Exactly!" he said. "Max isn't feeling so good, you see."

"My God," said Fifi. "Max is dying—is that it?"

"Not exactly dying," said Dooley. "Though he may not have long to live if this heat doesn't subside."

"I'm in," said Fifi immediately.

"But I haven't even told you what the mission is," said Dooley.

"I don't care. If I can be instrumental in saving Max's life, I'm definitely in. That cat has done so much for this community and for me personally that anything I can do to help him, I'll do gladly."

"Well, it's all about the kibble," he said, and proceeded to explain to her about the important mission he had in mind. A mission for which they needed a mastermind to think up a plan of campaign. The kind of mind that Max possessed but which was out of commission at that moment.

"You want me to save some kibble from destruction?" asked Fifi. She seemed a little less than impressed with his request.

"Not just any kibble," he said. "*The* kibble. The only kibble in the world."

"I don't know, Dooley," said Fifi. "Are you sure this is worth getting into trouble with your human over?"

He had thought about this very deeply, and so his response was both abrupt and forceful. "Absolutely. We have to save this kibble. These are the only two bags remaining in the whole wide world and we have to make sure they're saved for posterity."

"Okay, fine. If you think it's necessary…"

She wasn't as excited about the mission as he would have hoped, so he decided to use his ace. "Max has sanctioned the mission," he said. "Before he collapsed from heat exposure, he said, with his final breath, 'Ask Fifi,' and mentioned that if there's any pet that can do this, it's you."

Her smile was something to behold. "He said that, did he?"

"He did. You're the only one who can save the legendary Franklin Cooper's legacy, Fifi."

His words had touched a chord, for her sense that he was asking her to roll a large boulder up a particularly steep hill was replaced with a happy smile and a hint of that can-do attitude that was typical of the tiny but resourceful, brave, and clever Yorkie. "Okay, let's do it," she said. "Where did you say this kibble is right now?"

And so he explained to her where the kibble could be found. He also added that she had no less than three cats at her disposal to do any heavy lifting that needed to be done: himself, Brutus, and Harriet.

"Okay, just let me think for a moment," said Fifi and closed her eyes. Soaking in that paddling pool must have done her a world of good, Dooley thought, and for a brief moment wondered if he shouldn't try the same thing. But then he took one look at that water and decided against it. A lifelong aversion to getting wet can't be overcome in a second—not even when the fate of Franklin Cooper is at stake.

And so he waited patiently for Fifi to come up with a plan of campaign. He knew it would be a pippin, maybe not as good as any plan Max would have come up with, but a close second.

As he lay there, he sincerely hoped that Chase would deliver the goods in the form of a nice big fan so they could cool down Max's corpus. He now understood why a computer always has a built-in fan. All of that computing power needs to be cooled down at all times, and the same clearly applied to their beloved friend.

"I've got it!" suddenly Fifi yelled, and when Dooley glanced in her direction, he saw that she wasn't kidding, for he would have recognized that light in her eyes anywhere.

It was the same light he had seen so often in Max's eyes.

It was the light of intelligence when it hit upon a great idea!

CHAPTER 5

Freddie Tottman had been walking along the road when he experienced a funny sensation at the bottom of his feet. Either it was his rubber soles that were melting or it was the asphalt. Either way, it wasn't conducive to a pleasant state of mind. He had been sweating profusely now for the past hour or so, ever since he had ventured out of the waiting room of the doctor's office where he'd been ensconced for the better part of the morning.

It's never a fun experience to be seated in a doctor's waiting room, seeing as it usually means that there's something thoroughly wrong with you—perhaps even fatally so. The doctor had been nice enough, telling him that they had to await the results of the blood tests he had ordered from the lab, and that he shouldn't worry too much—at least not for now. That told him that he might have to worry later on, which isn't what anyone likes to hear.

Freddie walked on. He cursed himself for parking his car so far from the doctor's office, but then all the parking spaces had been taken, and he'd had to drive quite a few blocks to get rid of his vehicle. He finally reached his car and saw that he'd parked it right in front of an old and dilapidated structure. He hadn't noticed before, but the house wasn't congruent at all with the other houses that lined this particular neighborhood, which mostly appeared to consist of pleasant suburban dwellings. This house was different, though, in that it had definitely seen better days. The front garden was a tangle of weeds, and the building itself could use a lick of paint—or a demolition crew. And as he stood staring at it, he noticed a for-sale sign that had dropped off its perch and lay half-concealed behind a shrub.

He didn't know why, but for some reason, he felt compelled to snap a picture of the sign with his phone. It wasn't that he was necessarily in the market for a house, seeing as he lived rent-free at his parents' place. But lately, his folks had started making noises about him moving out, so he got the distinct impression that they wouldn't mind if their perennial student son would eventually get ready to stand on his own two feet and find a place of his own. And considering that this place looked as if it wouldn't cost an arm and a leg, it might be available within his price range, which was minuscule.

He had been working at Bread Baguette & Beyond, the popular bakery in town, for three months now while he awaited the results of a few job interviews he had done. As a mechanical engineer, he had fully expected that he'd have the job offers for the picking, but that hadn't been the case. Everywhere he had applied, they said they weren't hiring, and even though he was still maintaining an optimistic attitude, and so were his parents, he was starting to fear that he might not find his dream job anytime soon. Hence the job working the counter at their local bakery, whose owner was a friend of his mom's and had decided to do her old school chum a good turn by hiring her son.

He had a feeling she already regretted the decision,

though, and it had to be said that he wasn't exactly baker material. He didn't know one loaf of bread from the next, and frankly couldn't be bothered with how many calories a particular sandwich contained, or even if the gluten-intolerant, glucose-intolerant, and sodium-intolerant folks of this world could safely buy this bread or that. So if his blood work came back fine, he might be longer for this world but not much longer for the bakery, if his boss's last outburst was something to go on. Even though she later said she'd called him a 'loaf' as some form of endearment, he'd clearly understood 'loafer.' And maybe she was right. But then as long as he didn't land his dream job, anything else was simply a waste of his time.

He got into his old rust bucket of a car and would have driven off if he hadn't lightly tapped the car in front of him when he stuck his key into the ignition and discovered that he'd left the car in first. The engine stalled, and as he saw the car in front of him move, he quickly checked left and right, and behind him, only to find that there were no witnesses. And as he started maneuvering to get out of the cramped space he'd crammed himself in, suddenly there was a loud rap on his window. And when he looked up, he found himself gazing into the angry face of a woman of quite attractive aspect.

"You hit my car!" she exclaimed, quite audible through the closed window. And so despite his feeling he probably shouldn't, he rolled down his window to address the irate woman.

"I'm sorry," he said. "Did you say something?"

"I said you hit the rear of my car!"

"No, I didn't."

"I saw it move!"

"No, it didn't."

"You're saying I shouldn't believe my own eyes?"

"You could believe mine," he ventured. "And I can promise you that I didn't see a thing."

"That's probably because you're blind," she said, possibly referring to the thick glasses he wore and had worn ever since he was a boy of six, causing several of his classmates to refer to him from then on as Freddie Four-Eyes, which wasn't a very nice way to address anyone.

"Will you please get out of your car?" said the woman. "And we'll look at the damage together."

"There is no damage," he said. "Because I didn't hit your car. And now I'm afraid I must be off."

And he made to roll up his window again. But that was before she simply stuck her hand inside the door and then proceeded to yank it open and practically drag him out of his vehicle. He would have told a passing policeman that road rage was real, even with the female of the species, but of course there was no policeman anywhere in the vicinity. Where are they when you need them?

"Look," she said, as she positioned him in front of her car. "See that?"

He blankly stared in the direction she was pointing. "No, I don't."

"There! It's a scratch!"

"No, it's not."

"Yes, it is! You scratched the paint!"

"No, I didn't."

She produced a sound he would have described as 'Aaaaargh,' maybe, or 'Grrrrr!' or somewhere in between. And as she raised her arms, possibly in an attempt to strike, he also raised his, and as he did, somehow or other his fist connected with her chin. He watched as her eyes rolled up in her head and as she went down, made sure she didn't hit her head on the asphalt. For a moment he wondered if he should call an ambulance, but since he could only foresee a lot of trouble if he did, he simply positioned her on the sidewalk and decided that discretion is the better part of valor and got back into his car.

The last thing he needed was to be accused of causing damage to this crazy lady's car, and to the physical integrity of her person. Not when he had so much else going on in his life.

As he drove off, he wondered where he had seen her before. Though he sincerely hoped never to lay eyes on her again, so maybe it would be a good idea not to park his car on this particular street again for the time being. He might not have a very good memory for faces, but it was possible that she did.

CHAPTER 6

Rebekka Lipscombe woke up with a slight headache. For some odd reason, she found herself seated on the sidewalk, her back against her car, wondering what was going on. But as she gradually regained consciousness, suddenly she remembered, and she sat up with a jerk: that man!

She shouldn't have done that, for pain shot through her cranium, as if it was being subjected to thousands of little needles being stuck into her skull.

"Ouch," she groaned, and sat back down again. She didn't know what this guy had done to her, but he must have done something to make her feel this way. And as she tried to recollect the details of their fateful encounter, all she could think was that he must have struck her a nasty blow to the head the moment their interaction had turned unpleasant.

Once more, though more slowly this time, she raised herself up, and as she inspected the damage to her car that the man had caused, she decided it wasn't as bad as she had thought. Just a minor scratch. Nothing that couldn't be fixed by an experienced mechanic. She now wondered why she had created such a hullabaloo over such a small thing. It was true, though, that she had been in a more volatile state of mind lately, owing to the fact that her mother was in the hospital—she had just returned from visiting her—and that her dad relied mostly on her to supply him with the necessary groceries so he could keep on living by himself. The pressure had been considerable, as she also had to deal with her own family who needed her, as well as a pretty demanding job that took a lot out of her.

All in all, the pressure had been building gradually, and so she very much doubted if she would have reacted the way she had even six months ago.

That didn't excuse that cretin of a man from knocking her out, of course. And she vowed to give him a piece of her mind if she ever bumped into him again.

For a moment, she considered going to the police, but then decided against it. She had enough on her plate without having to spend half a day at the police station filling out forms and answering a lot of questions. And what would be the upshot? That the guy got a slap on the wrist? She definitely had better things to do with her time. And so she got behind the wheel and drove off. In her haste to get out of the hospital and then run a few errands, she had totally forgotten to pick up a present for her niece's birthday, something she needed to remedy posthaste, lest she incur her sister's ire—something no one in the family liked to provoke.

She was driving back into town when she thought she saw the same car that had bumped into hers, and as she passed by, she saw the same man who had knocked her out!

And in spite of her vow not to waste more time on the incident, she stomped her foot on the brake, then put the car in reverse. And as she drew level with the guy and looked across, she was gratified to see that he slowly turned his head, and when he saw her, his face actually turned a little pale, and his expression morphed from one of complacent self-indulgence to one of abject horror and dismay.

She gave him a little wave. And since he couldn't get out of the car since she was blocking the door, instead, he quickly crawled across the gearshift and got out through the passenger-side door.

"Christ," she said as she watched him take off hurriedly along the sidewalk, putting some distance between himself and what he must consider his nemesis but who was, in actual fact, his unfortunate victim.

She quickly parallel-parked right behind the man's car and also got out. Scanning the shops along Main Street, she couldn't see him, as he had disappeared into the crowd.

It would take her too long to find him and confront him about what he'd done, but what she could do was take a picture of his license plate, just in case she did find the time to drop by the police station.

She just hoped he wouldn't return before she did and do more damage to her car. If he was the vindictive type, he just might.

And since she was close to the toy store located two stores down from the General Store, she popped in to buy her niece the present she had in mind and tried to put the entire incident out of her mind.

* * *

Felix Bennett watched the woman walk into his store and hoped she would put in a pretty large order. He could use the money, since for some reason people seemed to have stopped using his store as a source for all their toy needs. Presumably, they had shifted their business to the mall, where several large-chain toy stores could be found that offered everything people needed, especially the big brands, whereas he liked to offer the smaller boutique toy store stuff. It had always worked for him before but seemed to work for him less now, even though he'd been in business for closing in on fifteen years now.

He waited a moment before approaching the customer and offered his services in finding what she needed. When she told him she needed to buy something for her niece, who was ten years old, he immediately shifted into full salesman mode and before long had guided her in the direction of the kind of toys ten-year-olds liked today. It was his great pride and joy always to find for his customers what they needed, and not what he needed to shift, like some of the bigger chains seemed to do.

The customer, whose name was Rita Watts, was extremely grateful, and after he had offered her a customer card and a discount, he wrapped up the present—a nice purple dragon with assorted wizardry items belonging to the fictional world of witchcraft that a very creative designer he personally knew had created—and would have sent her on her way if a man hadn't entered the store carrying a firearm and threatening to shoot him if he didn't deliver the contents of his cash register pronto.

The man didn't look all that sane, and immediately he suspected he was high on some illegal substance. Possibly Plakka, the new designer drug that was all the rage in drug addict circles. The woman looked terrified, and even though it had been a while since he'd last been subjected to this kind of threat, he also felt a sort of terror rising in his throat like bile. But what he felt even more than fear was a sense of righteous anger. And so the moment the man glanced over to the entrance to the store, he took the dragon he had been wrapping up in gift wrap and hit it over the man's head. The dragon's tail, which was made of metal, penetrated the man's temple, and immediately he went down like a ton of bricks.

As he watched him drop to the floor, he saw the dragon was actually sticking out of his head like a flag.

"Oh, dear," he said as he brought a distraught hand to his mouth. "Now why did I go and do that?"

"I think he's dead," said Rita. She looked up at him in horror. "I think you killed him!"

"I think you may be right," he said. Then he thought quick. It was self-defense, of course, and this woman would attest to that for sure. But it would also mean a lot of paperwork and a lot of nonsense and trouble. They might even try to pin this whole thing on him and accuse him of manslaughter. He might even have to go to prison, or at the very least get some kind of criminal record, even if he found a lawyer who could get him off—but then where would he find the money to pay for such a lawyer?

And so in that split second when he had to decide how to proceed, he decided to handle things a little differently. And so he walked around the counter, knelt down next to the robber, picked up his weapon, and pointed it at the customer. "I'm going to get rid of this body, and you're going to help me," he said, surprised at his own sangfroid. "Is that clear?"

Rita nodded quickly, and at his instigation grabbed the man by the feet while he grabbed him by the hands. Together they dragged him the length of the store and into the storeroom at the back.

"I can't afford to go to prison," he explained.

"No, of course not," said Rita, who looked terrified, which was understandable. She had come into his store to buy a present for her ten-year-old niece and instead had gotten roped into covering up a murder. Though technically it was self-defense, not murder.

"I don't have the money for a lawyer," he added, feeling a need to explain himself to this customer, who looked like a perfectly nice person.

"No, I understand," she said, even though from her haunted expression, she couldn't wait to get as far away from him as possible, so she was probably simply humoring him.

"If I go to prison now, I'll have to close my store, and I'll go bust."

"But surely the police will understand that it was self-defense?" she argued.

"The police aren't as lenient as you might think. A colleague of mine who runs a jewelry store was robbed last year. The thieves smashed all the display cases in his store and knocked him over the head. So when he got the chance, he grabbed the shotgun he had concealed underneath his counter and managed to squeeze off one shot at the robbers as they fled the scene. One of them was killed instantly, while his colleague managed to get away. And do you know what happened? The dead man's family filed a complaint against him, and they won! So now he's looking at actual jail time for manslaughter, plus he has to pay damages to the dead robber's family while that one robber still got away with most of the loot, and his business went bust." He shook his head decidedly. "I don't want the same thing to happen to me. I've worked too hard to build up my business."

Was it simply his imagination or was her expression becoming a little more understanding?

"I get it," she said. "Things aren't always fair, are they? Take me, for instance. I was just knocked over the head by a man who bumped into my car and scratched the paint. I should go to the police, but knowing that I'll spend hours in there filling out paperwork only to see the man getting a slap on the wrist, or maybe not even that, makes me figure it's just not worth it. So I decided to let him go."

He stared at her and thought she was a lot feistier than he had given her credit for. "You want to get even with this guy?" he asked, out of sheer curiosity.

She thought for a moment. "I guess so. He did hurt me, and my sense of justice tells me I shouldn't let him get away with it."

"Too right you shouldn't let him get away with that," he said.

They had reached the back door leading to the little courtyard behind the store. "Let's put him out there," he suggested. He hadn't really thought this through, so he had no idea what he was going to do with the body.

"You could always drag the body out tonight," Rita suggested, showing that her mind was running along the same lines as his. "And dump him in the canal. Or maybe stuff him in a dumpster. Or you could bury him in the woods. Chances are no one will ever find him there."

"I hadn't thought about the woods," he said. "That's a great idea. Rita, is it?"

"That's right. You can't do it yourself, though, can you? It probably takes two people to shift this body, as he's pretty heavy. Do you have someone who can help you bury him?"

He shook his head. "I have my mother, but she's old and not really in a position to help me shift bodies and bury them in the woods. Plus, she wouldn't like it. No, I'll just have to do it myself."

"I could help you," she suggested, causing him to give her a look of suspicion.

"What do you mean?"

"I could help you bury him." The way she was looking at him, with no guile in her eyes whatsoever made him wonder if she was for real.

"Now why would you do that?" he asked.

She shrugged. "Because I don't think it's fair that you'd be the victim of a robbery and you would get the blame for acting in self-defense. Same thing as me with this guy who hit me."

"So… what are you suggesting?" he asked, still not fully understanding what was going on here.

She took a deep breath. "If I help you get rid of this body, will you help me get back at the guy that did this to me?" She raised her head and showed him a bruise that was forming on her chin. "I don't know what he did, but he must have used some considerable force, cause I passed out for a while."

"He must have given you an uppercut," he guessed.

"He shouldn't have done that, should he?"

"No, he definitely shouldn't," said Felix.

"So will you help me? Get even?"

He thought for a moment, and as he regarded her closely, saw no signs of subterfuge. So he finally nodded. "Okay. If you help me get rid of this body, I'll help you get back at the guy that did that to you."

She smiled and held out her hand. "Deal."

"Deal," he confirmed, and they shook hands on it.

It was a great relief, for he hadn't really wanted to hurt this woman. She was a witness, and logic told him that if he was going to survive this incident unscathed he should get rid of her. But since he wasn't a professional killer, that was the last thing he wanted. It was still possible she was just saying these things to double-cross him later on, and turn him into the police, but something told him that wasn't the case. Call it a hunch, but after having run his store for fifteen years he had developed a lot of psychological insight into his customers, and something told him that this woman was on the level.

CHAPTER 7

Cliff Puckering didn't like this one bit. After he'd already written several times to Town Hall and also the police station, these vandals still kept dealing their drugs in the little street behind his house. From his upstairs window, he had a perfect view of them as they gathered there and drove around on their motorcycles, deal drugs, and made a mess of things. Every time he called the police station, they told him the same thing: they'd send a patrol car to check on things. But since he watched out for that patrol car, he knew full well that no patrol car was ever sent. So, they simply lied to him! Used his hard-earned tax money to do nothing at all to protect the citizenry against these horrible hooligans.

He could see them now as he looked out of his window. They knew where he lived, and they laughed at him, held up their hands, and gave him rude gestures.

"Oh, for crying out loud!" he said as he retreated his head to the safety of his pleasant little home.

"Don't go crazy up there!" his wife Mindy shouted from downstairs.

He carefully navigated the stairs and joined her in the living room. "It's those kids again," he said. "Now they're spraying graffiti on the back wall of Lester's place."

"Well, let them," said Mindy, who was probably a lot more sensible than he was. "As long as they don't spray their graffiti on our back wall, it's all fine with me."

"But they shouldn't do that," he said. "If they keep this up they're going to defile all of our homes, and then the value of our property will plummet, and then where are we?"

"We're not going to sell up and move out of here any time soon, are we?" she asked as he let himself drop down into his comfortable armchair. "So what are you so worried about?"

"I'm worried that they won't limit themselves to using spray paint," he said gloomily as he picked up the TV Guide and checked what was on television tonight. "That they'll start breaking into places and steal things. They are using drugs, you know. I can see them. Using and dealing drugs."

"So?"

"So, they'll need money to pay for those drugs. And guess where they're going to find it?"

"Oh, I wouldn't worry too much about it if I were you," said his wife of fifty years as she picked up her knitting and recommenced work on the sweater she had been knitting for their two granddaughters Kitty and Nina. "It's bad for your ticker, and anyway, there's nothing you can do about it, is there?"

"I guess not," he said. He'd called the police several times. He'd written letters to the mayor and to the several council members. "Unless I go out there myself," he suggested.

She smiled. "You're not going to do that, Cliff." It wasn't a question but a statement, and he knew she was right. Once upon a time he might have been a force to be reckoned with, a real bruiser who intimidated people by the sheer force of his imposing presence, but the years hadn't been kind to him, and he was nothing but a shadow of his former self now. If he went out there and faced off against those hooligans, things might not end well for him. He might even end up in the hospital or worse.

"No, I guess you're right," he said finally. And by all rights, he knew he should let the matter rest. It wasn't up to him to take matters into his own hands. He wasn't some kind of avenging angel. He was just a regular citizen and should probably abide by the law like any other citizen. But as he sank a little deeper into his armchair, he couldn't help but wonder if there wasn't more he could do.

"Turn on the TV, will you?" said Mindy. "I want to watch that new cooking show."

And so he turned on the television. They hadn't been out of the house for days now, owing to that heatwave. Luckily for them, their son James had outfitted the house with a stellar air conditioning system that kept things cool without causing them to catch a cold, so they had been spared the worst of the heat. And if the weather forecast was to be believed, the weather was about to turn. It would probably end with a nice big storm, and soon after, things would go back to normal again.

Maybe that was the reason those kids were behaving so brazenly: maybe they were also affected by the heat. Hadn't he read an article recently that said that most murders happened in the summer, owing to the fact that the heat brought out the worst in people? So maybe when things cooled down, it would have a cooling effect on those thugs, and they would finally stop making such a nuisance of themselves.

He channel-surfed for a while, in search of that cooking show Mindy wanted to watch, and happened to hit a Dirty Harry movie. For a moment, he watched Mr. Eastwood confront some lowlife.

He pondered the situation they found themselves in. And then suddenly he flashed on an idea. It was probably a crazy idea, but as it took hold of him and refused to let go, he was starting to see that it just might be the best idea he'd had in quite a while.

He got up while Mindy was engrossed in her program, grabbed his phone from the cabinet, and dialed a number he was intimately familiar with. It wasn't long before a familiar voice sounded in his ear.

"Cliff? What's wrong?"

"Father Reilly," he said. "You're still a member of that neighborhood watch, aren't you?"

"That's right. Why? Do you have a problem we need to look at?"

He steeled his resolve. "I want in."

"What do you mean, you want in?"

"I want to join the neighborhood watch."

"I'm not sure we're taking on new recruits," said the priest.

"I don't care. I need to do something or else I'll go crazy." And he explained about the young punks making his life and that of his neighbors a living hell, and the blatant refusal by the police and the town council to do anything about it. "So you see, I want to make this neighborhood safe again, and the only way to do it is by joining the neighborhood watch and doing it myself."

"I see," said Father Reilly carefully, as was his habit. "Well, I hope you understand that we're not exactly a gang of vigilantes, Cliff. We patrol the streets, yes, but when we see something untoward, we simply report it to the police, and they intervene. We don't actually arrest people ourselves, or are even instrumental in approaching the criminals in any way, shape, or form."

"But I just told you: the police won't step in. I've called

them many times, and they promise to send a patrol car, but they never do. It's almost as if they simply don't care about us."

"No, I can see how that must be extremely disappointing," said the priest pensively.

"I want to do something, Father," he said. "Just sitting here twiddling my thumbs while my neighborhood goes up in flames is driving me nuts. I mean, isn't there anything I can do?"

For a moment, silence reigned on the other side of the line. It stretched out so long that Cliff thought that the priest had simply hung up on him.

"Hello?" he said. "Are you still there?"

"I'm still here," said Francis.

"So what do you think?"

"I think I'm going to run this by the neighborhood watch's leader," said the priest finally.

"Oh, but I thought you were the leader? Or is it Wilbur Vickery?"

"No, the real leader of the watch is Vesta Muffin."

He groaned. "God, no." He immediately realized his faux pas and corrected himself. "I'm sorry. I didn't mean to take the name of the Lord in vain, Father."

"That's all right. I know that Vesta is an acquired taste. But she's also very committed to the mission statement of the neighborhood watch. And not afraid to color outside the lines if need be. So I'll take it up with her, and I'll let you know what she decides."

He remembered that he'd once had a run-in with Vesta at the senior center, and so all hope that he would be admitted to her neighborhood watch, which he hadn't even known was hers, fled. "Fine," he said, experiencing a sinking feeling in the pit of his stomach.

"Buck up, Cliff," said the priest, who had a sixth sense for a parishioner's sense of despair. "For what it's worth, I'll throw the full weight of my endorsement behind your candidacy."

"Thanks, Father," he said. For all the good it would do. And as he glanced out of the window, he saw that some of the youths that had been making such a nuisance of themselves had discovered that his car was one of the few ones on the block that still had an actual antenna sticking out of it—it was that old. And, of course, that antenna exacted such a powerful appeal to them they just had to attach themselves to it and snap it off. He watched as they howled with fun and ran the whole length of the street holding it up like a trophy, before shoving it into the mailbox of one of his neighbors.

His hands itched to lay them on these little mongrels' necks and snap them like twigs.

CHAPTER 8

To state that Franklin Cooper wasn't a happy camper would be an understatement of the highest order. As he gazed out of the window of his small, cramped room at the Edith Wale Retirement Community, he wondered what his son would be doing at that moment. Not to mention his son's wife Melanie and their two kids—his grandchildren. Even though Franklin Jr. had told the court a couple of years previously that he wouldn't have anything more to do with his dad, Franklin Sr. hadn't really believed he'd go through with this. In truth, he thought that his son's lawyer had simply suggested this as a legal technique to get him off the hook and deny that he had anything to do with the business that his dad had operated for all those many years. Quite possibly the most popular brand of pet food in the land, until that fateful day three years ago when certain things had been brought to the attention of the FDA, and the hammer had come down. There had been reports in the media, and a court case, and in the end his empire had come tumbling down and had crumbled into dust.

But to think that his son would deny him access to his

grandkids was something he never would have expected from him. And he was sure that Melanie didn't agree with any of it. To deny a grandfather access to his grandchildren was simply cruel. Especially since he didn't feel as if he'd done anything to deserve such a fate. It had been months now since he'd been admitted to the nursing home, and he still hadn't received any visits. And since his health was deteriorating fast, he might never see the girls again before he died, which didn't bear thinking about—which was probably why it was all he did. All day, every day.

Once a millionaire many times over, and the most feted pet food producer in the country, now he was forgotten by all, and tucked away in a small room in this nursing home, with the government footing the bill since he was pretty much broke.

He studied the scenery outside of his window, and wondered if it was as hot out there as they said it was on the news. A heatwave was allegedly ravaging the county. Lucky for him they had a wonderfully potent AC system installed at the home he was staying at, and that sufficed to keep things at a comfortable temperature. He watched as a small tweety bird perched in a tree in the piece of land he overlooked from his window. He took out his binoculars and studied it carefully, a smile creasing his face. Too long he had worked like a dog. His workaholic habits had cost him his marriage and the relationship with his son and daughter, which is probably why he found it very gratifying that now, in his old age, he had so much time on his hands he could study the birds in the small nature reserve located behind the nursing home from morning till night and never get tired of it. It was better than anything on television, which is why he rarely watched. Too depressing and upsetting in his view. The only channel he did watch was the Discovery Channel. At least you could always learn something new.

He returned to his chair and let himself drop into it with a groan. And as he did, suddenly he noticed that he had received a new message on his phone. Frowning, he picked the device up from the small table next to his armchair. And as he put on his reading glasses, he saw that the message was sent by Patsy Cooper. His heart lodging in his throat from pure excitement, he clicked on the message to open it. And as he read the message his granddaughter had written, a smile lifted the corners of his mouth.

'Hi, Grandpa. Daddy doesn't want me to write to you, but our schoolteacher told us that it is very important to honor our grandparents on Grandparents' Day, so I wanted to write you to say hi and ask you if you could come to my school to speak. We're all supposed to bring one of our grandparents and introduce them to the rest of the class. So I wanted to ask you to come to my school so I can introduce you to my friends. Just don't tell Mommy and Daddy, because they won't like it. Patsy Cooper.'

Tears rolled down his cheeks as he looked up. Was it possible? Looked like it was. And so he immediately wrote back and said that he would be happy to be present at Patsy's school for Grandparents' Day. 'Just tell me the time and place, and I will be there,' he wrote. With bells on!

* * *

FRANKLIN COOPER JR. got a ping on his phone and glanced down at the device. Even though strictly speaking he wasn't allowed to use his mobile at work, he still kept it in his drawer, like most of his colleagues. It seemed like an outdated policy that they couldn't use their phones. What if something happened to one of the girls? Or maybe Melanie urgently needing to get a hold of him? But then their bosses maybe didn't have kids of their own, otherwise they wouldn't insist on enforcing such a silly rule.

He glanced down at his phone and saw that his wife was trying to reach him. So he glanced left and right to make sure that his supervisor wasn't anywhere in the vicinity. Arnold might be old-fashioned but that didn't make him near-sighted. That man had eyes in the back of his head and always knew and saw all. He seemed to have gone to the bathroom, though, for Franklin couldn't see the man anywhere. So he quickly opened the message and stared at it.

'Patsy has invited your dad to the school's Grandparents' Day,' Cindy wrote.

He inwardly cursed. He'd known that this day would come. They couldn't protect the girls from their granddad forever, especially as they got older. They had begun asking a lot of questions about Franklin Sr. lately, and it had become increasingly difficult to fend off their curiosity about why they weren't allowed to have any contact with their grandfather.

Before he could text her back, Arnold entered the office floor again, his eyes peeled for any sign of subterfuge or neglect of the rules the company of Edmund McFall & Co liked to instill on its underlings. They might be in the agriculture tire-producing business and a national powerhouse of the highest order, but that didn't stop them from treating their workers like babies.

Once again, he cursed the day the FDA had closed down the family plant and had reduced the entire Cooper family to begging for scraps on the job market. Though he cursed his dad even more, of course, since it had been his fault in the first place. Going from a junior director at one of the most prestigious and successful pet product companies to the breadline in the space of a couple of weeks had been brutal, and having to sell his home and take the girls out of their private school and jeopardizing their future even more so. But he couldn't explain that to Patsy and Tamara. They were too young to understand.

He vowed to get in touch with his dad for the first time in years and tell the old man that he should stop trying to worm his way into the family again. If they couldn't stop the girls from trying to get in touch with their grandfather, they could stop him from answering their calls or their texts. And if he needed to take him to court again to accomplish that, so be it.

He suddenly became aware that Arnold was staring at him intently, and realized he'd been gazing idly out of the window instead of at his computer where his main job was to input the data of the safety reports so they could ensure their customers that Edmund McFall tires were the best on the market and the safest option to put on all of their tractors, combines, sprayers and skid-steer loaders.

Arnold pointed two fingers at his own eyes and then in Franklin's direction, to indicate that he was watching him. Franklin bowed his head and continued his soul-crushing work. He knew he should be grateful to have found a job at all, after having been taken to court in the aftermath of the demise of the family business, but even after three years he still found it hard to get used to having to work for a boss and not being in charge of his own fate. He was tired of tires, that's what it boiled down to, and blamed it all on his dad.

He wondered how Patsy had managed to get in touch with her granddad, and even though he didn't approve, secretly he was proud of her resourcefulness in finding a way to contact the old man.

CHAPTER 9

Max was still on the floor where Dooley had left him. For a moment, he was afraid that his friend had stopped breathing, but when he put his nose to the big cat's lips and sniffed, he discovered with a happy heart that Max hadn't expired from the heat but was still alive.

"Max," he said softly, not wanting to cause his friend even more distress than he was already feeling. "Max, it's Dooley. I've asked Fifi to help us get that kibble to safety, and she's promised that she will. She hasn't come up with a plan yet, but I'm sure it's just a matter of time." He eyed his friend for a response, but when no response was forthcoming, he carried on. "Unless you have hit on something?" Still no reaction. "I mean, Fifi's mind is great, but she's very small, and so I'm thinking that her brain must also be very small. The size of a tennis ball, maybe. Or maybe a ping-pong ball? But your brain?" He gestured to his friend's magnificently large head. "Well, your brain should probably be in the Guinness Book of Records. I'll bet it's the size of a cantaloupe. Maybe even a watermelon or a giant pumpkin."

Still nothing stirred. Max hadn't even opened his eyes to respond to Dooley's little speech. Those who had been listening were Harriet and Brutus, who now descended the stairs into the basement and joined them.

"Still out like a light, huh?" said Brutus. He shook his head. "If Chase doesn't show up with that fan, I fear the worst, you guys."

"Oh, no!" said Dooley, biting his lower lip. "Not... death!"

Brutus nodded mournfully. "It's very well possible. People have died from the heat, you know, and there's absolutely no reason to suggest that cats can't suffer the same fate. In fact, cats are probably worse off since we don't sweat through our pores, so we have a much harder time cooling off. We sweat through our paws, of course, but compared to the rest of his body, Max's paws are tiny—very tiny."

"We should probably tell Odelia that Max is about to die," said Harriet as she cast a sad look at their friend. "I mean, just look at him. I could cry."

She did look as if she could burst into tears any moment, Dooley thought, and since watching someone cry is very infectious, it wasn't long before he was crying buckets himself.

It was at that moment that a familiar voice spoke. "Can't you guys go and be sad somewhere else? You're interrupting a very nice nap."

It was Max, and as Dooley's heart lifted, he saw that his friend was looking at them intently, a smile playing about his lips.

"Max, you're alive!" he said.

"Of course I'm alive. This concrete is very nice and cool, I have to say. Spend about half an hour down here, and you're right as rain." He glanced up at the ceiling. "Is it still so hot out?"

"It's incredibly hot," said Harriet. "Inhumane." She clasped her arms around Max's neck. "Oh, am I glad that you're not dead, Max. I don't know what I would have done if you were."

In spite of the fact that Brutus didn't like it when his girlfriend hugged and kissed other cats, he didn't seem annoyed this time. Possibly that was because he was hugging and kissing Max himself! Max didn't seem to like all of these physical displays of affection, though.

"I'm fine!" he insisted. "I can't believe you'd think there was anything the matter with me."

"Don't go up there, Max," said Brutus. "You won't like it."

"No, I think I'll stay down here myself for the time being," said Harriet. "And only come out again once the sun has gone down and the world stops feeling like an oven turned up high."

"So what's the news on the kibble front?" asked Max as he yawned.

"Like I said, Fifi is on the case," said Dooley. "She said she was going to try and think up some solution, so I trust that she will."

"Fifi is a spent force," said Brutus. "She'll never be able to come up with anything, mark my words."

"So how about you, Max?" asked Harriet. "Have you come up with a plan?"

"It's easy," said Max. "We wait until Chase and Odelia have gone to bed and then we spring into action. We grab those bags of kibble and hide them—easy peasy."

"Where should we hide them?" asked Brutus.

"Where Odelia won't come looking," said Max. "And what is the only place in the house where Odelia is most likely never to go?" He waited for their response, even though it was clear that none of them had the answer, except himself, of course. "The attic! She doesn't like to go up there for reasons that are unclear to me."

He was right. As long as they had known Odelia, Dooley had never known her to go up to the attic. The problem was that they'd have a pretty hard time dragging two bags of kibble all the way up to that attic, as it was one of those spaces only accessible by pulling down a wooden folding ladder. And since cats aren't exactly equipped with the required digits to carry out such an intricate and delicate operation, they would need a human accomplice to accomplish that daring feat of derring-do. But when they suggested to Max that it couldn't be done, he waved their objections away.

"Gran will do it, no sweat."

"Gran? You want to ask her?" said Harriet.

"Why would Gran help us hide two bags of kibble?" asked Brutus.

"Because in return, we'll accompany her on her patrols for a couple of nights, contrary to our promise never to set foot in her car ever again."

Since Gran had a habit of trying to rope them into accompanying her on her nocturnal neighborhood watch trips, and it was hard for them to say no, they had been in the car with her on many of those trips, and it often didn't end well. Like the time they had been caught breaking into a home that Gran thought had been burgled by a thief but ended up being the homeowner having forgotten his keys and crawling over the fence to break into his own home. He hadn't enjoyed the company of the watch, and being the subject of a citizen's arrest by Gran and her cronies and had even filed a complaint against them. And since the man owned no less than two large dogs, and he had thought of nothing better to do than to sic them on the four cats, they'd had to run for their lives that time. After that, they'd sworn a solemn oath never to join Gran on her adventures ever again. Until now.

"Okay, so maybe she'll go for it," said Brutus. "But have you thought about what this means for us, Max? We'll have to sit in that car again for hours on end, and forego cat choir for nights in a row."

"A small price to pay to lay our paws on the best cat kibble ever made," Max argued.

"I guess so," said Brutus dubiously. He then cast a glance at Dooley. "You said saving two bags of Franklin Cooper kibble, but I thought there were three?"

"Odelia managed to destroy one bag," said Dooley sadly, "and threw it in the trash."

"Threw it in the trash!" Harriet cried, aghast at the thought of the best kibble in the world languishing in the trash. "But why?"

"Because it had been on the floor, and she doesn't want us eating food from the floor. Claims it is bad for us."

"This can't be happening," said Harriet as she clasped her whiskers. "We have to save that kibble!"

"Harriet is right," said Brutus. "Franklin Cooper kibble can't be in the trash. That's akin to sacrilege. We have to make sure it's saved from such a terrible fate, you guys!"

Dooley felt that Harriet and Brutus had a point. The problem was that Odelia wouldn't like it if they rooted around in the trash. She might even get very upset with them. Lately, he felt that their human hadn't been in the best of moods, and this would only serve to exacerbate that.

But Max seemed to agree that they needed to do something, and so a plan was made. They wouldn't simply rope Gran into helping them stash that kibble in the attic, but also to save those pellets of delicious cat food from the trash. In other words: a bold and audacious plan!

CHAPTER 10

Odelia had been waiting patiently for her husband to arrive home. Frankly speaking, she could have done with a few fans herself. At the office, the temperature had been doable since it was an old building with thick walls and small windows, and Dan had had the foresight a long time ago to install a couple of ceiling fans that did a lot to mitigate the heat. But at home, it was frankly unbearable, and she worried not only about her cats but also about Grace. The little girl's cheeks were red, and she looked sweaty.

"Daddy will be home soon," she said as she picked the little girl up and placed her next to the kitchen sink, where she had filled the basin with cold water. She now placed the little girl into the sink with her feet in the water and watched as she enjoyed the feel of the cooling water on her little feet. And as Odelia put her hands in, she appreciated the effect it had on her. They could have used the paddling pool, but the problem was that the sun was still out in full force, and they didn't have any shade at all. Not until Chase fixed the big umbrella and they could shade off that entire area of the backyard.

The sliding glass door opened and closed, and her husband walked in, looking remarkably cool in a pair of jeans and a crisp white shirt. She didn't understand how, but the heat never seemed to affect him. According to him, it was because he worked out so much, and his body was used to handling the heat much better because of that.

"Did you bring that fan?" she asked.

"I did," he said, holding up a large box. "And I also got one of those portable AC units. That should keep things nice and frosty in here from now on."

She gave him a grateful smile, and as he returned to the car to pick up the unit, she installed the fan and turned it on. Immediately, she felt the effect of the redistribution of air by the device. And so she opened the door to the basement further and yelled, "Max, Dooley! The fan is here!"

Immediately, there was the sound of stumbling paws on the stairs, and as four cats came hurrying up, she proudly pointed to the device. "Look at that!"

"Oh, this is so great!" said Dooley, and immediately got in front of the thing, allowing it to blow his fur this way and that. "I like it," he announced immediately.

"Isn't that dangerous?" asked Harriet. "I mean, too much wind is bad for you, isn't it? We could get a cold."

They all laughed at that. "With these temperatures, it's probably very difficult to catch a cold," Odelia told her cat.

"Fine," Harriet grudgingly allowed. "I'll give it five minutes. But if I start coughing and sneezing, I'll tell Vena it's all your fault." She glanced around, and when she caught sight of a piece of kibble that Odelia had neglected to sweep up, immediately dove at it and snapped it up, gobbling it up in seconds.

"You shouldn't eat that," said Odelia. "It's been on the floor."

"I don't care," said Harriet. "It's Franklin Cooper. It's the best in the world!"

"Still," said Odelia. "I don't even know if it's still good." She had intended to look at the expiration date on those bags the cats had dug up in the pantry but had totally forgotten. So she opened the kitchen cupboard now and took a look. And, of course, it was as she had expected. "This kibble has expired," she announced. "Years ago, in fact."

The look of horror on her cats' faces was something to behold.

"Years ago?" said Harriet. "That can't be right."

"It says so right here," said Odelia, pointing to the date on the bag. And so she took the bag, ripped it open, and deposited its contents into the trashcan.

A loud howl of anguish rose up from four throats as she did.

"Odelia, the best cat kibble in the world!" Harriet yelled.

"Please don't throw it away!" Max urged.

"We can eat it," said Dooley. "We'll eat it all."

"Expiration dates are only a guideline!" said Brutus.

"I'm sorry, you guys," said Odelia as she grabbed the second bag and checked the date. "I can't risk you getting sick from eating food that's past its expiration date." It was as she thought. Both bags had the same date, since they probably had been bought together. And so she tipped the contents of this final bag into the trash, just like the rest.

"At least throw it on the compost heap!" Max implored.

She pointed at her cat. "You're absolutely right," she said. "I shouldn't throw this in the trash when it should go in the compost." And so she dragged the bag from the trashcan and walked out of the kitchen to deliver it to her dad so he could throw it on his compost heap. The four cats followed her, but she prevented them from doing so. "You guys have to keep an eye on Grace for me," she said, reminding them of an oath they had sworn to make sure Grace never came to any harm.

"Oh, all right!" said Dooley, looking as sad as she had ever seen him. Clearly, this cat food meant a lot to them. But since it had been bought years ago, she couldn't in good conscience feed it to them. Who knows what might have proliferated in those bags by now. Maybe it was full of bugs, or worse, some kind of fungus. And so she took it to her dad, who was in the kitchen next door, staring out of the window with a dreamy look on his face while he was munching on a peanut butter sandwich.

"Should you be eating that right before dinner?" she asked. "You're going to spoil your appetite."

He looked up, as if waking up from deep thought. "Mh? Oh, hi, honey. What's that?"

"A bag of cat kibble," she said. "Expired, unfortunately. Can you dump it on your compost?"

"Of course," he said. "But don't let your mother see it," he warned. "She doesn't like it that I keep feeding that compost heap. Thinks it attracts vermin and sooner or later they'll make their way into the house."

"I won't tell her if you don't," she said with a smile. Mom often worried that creepy-crawly things might invade her personal space, and she was like a lioness in defending against it.

"Hot, isn't it?" said her dad, making a face. "You wouldn't believe the number of people suffering from the heat. Three heat-related deaths in the last twenty-four hours. High time the weather turned."

"You have AC at the office, don't you, Dad?"

"Oh, sure. But my patients don't always have the benefit of an AC unit, and a lot of them are suffering, especially the elderly ones. Only this morning I had to admit a patient to the hospital for heat-related issues. I'm not sure he'll make it through the night."

"Well, at least we're all doing fine." She glanced at her grandmother who now came walking into the kitchen clutching her phone and wearing a deep frown on her face. "How are you coping, Gran?"

Gran looked up. "Oh, fine, fine. A little bit of heat won't stop me from doing what must be done."

She shared a smile with her dad. "And what is that?" she asked.

"Oh, just this new member who wants to apply for the watch. I'm not sure I should allow him to join up. He's been a right pain in the patootie for years."

"Do I know him?" asked Dad.

"Not sure. Cliff Puckering?"

"Rings a bell," said Dad, nodding. "Retired foreman?"

"That's right. Used to work at the Franklin Cooper plant. Until it was closed down by the FDA."

Odelia frowned. "The Franklin Cooper plant was shut down by the FDA?"

"Sure. Don't you remember? There was a big hullabaloo. In the end, they were sued over violations of safety measures. Turned out they hadn't taken the correct precautions." She shook her head. "Too bad, since the cats loved that kibble. Said it was the best they'd ever had, and they absolutely adored it."

"I found a couple of bags in the pantry," said Odelia. "But they're expired, so I asked Dad to put them on the compost heap. The cats weren't happy."

"No, I imagine they weren't," said Gran. "Like I said, they were crazy about the stuff. Couldn't stop eating it and kept begging for more. Which told me that there was probably something wrong with it even before the FDA carried out its investigation."

"So what was wrong with it?" asked Dad as he took a few nuggets of the famous kibble out of his daughter's trash bag and rolled them around between his fingers before taking a sniff.

"Don't eat them, Tex," Gran advised. "I don't know what was wrong with them. That was never disclosed. We all hoped it would come out in the trial, but the Cooper family made a deal with the prosecution, and the case never went to court, and the evidence was sealed." She pointed to Odelia. "Dan wrote a couple of articles about the scandal. You should ask him. He'll remember."

Odelia didn't think it was that important to bother her editor about. She pointed to the bag. "Just get rid of it, will you, Dad?"

"I will do it right now," said Dad, and despite Gran's admonition, he still gave that piece of kibble a lick. He made a face. "Yuck! Tastes horrible."

"I told you not to put it in your mouth, you naughty boy!" said Gran.

"It's fine, Gran," said Odelia. "Everyone knows that expiration dates are only a guideline," she added with a grin, remembering a line the cats had given her.

"I know, but like I said, we never got to find out what was in that kibble," said Gran. "For all we know, they could have put actual poison in there, and pets could have died."

Odelia gulped, and so did Dad, who quickly spat out the kibble in the sink.

Just then, Mom entered the kitchen, and when she saw the bag in her husband's hands, asked, "Putting out the trash, honey?"

"That's right," said Dad, giving his wife an innocent face. "In fact I'll do it right now."

"Good," Mom murmured as she opened the fridge to start

dinner prep. "Are you and Chase joining us for dinner?" she asked.

"Sounds good," said Odelia. She didn't mind cooking, but after a long day at the office, it was the last thing she wanted to do right now. At least not all by herself. "I'll go and look in on Chase," she said. "And pick up Grace, and then I'll join you guys, all right?"

Moments later, she was home again and watching as her husband tried to get the portable AC unit he had picked up to work. "I got it from a colleague," he said as he scratched his head. "She said it was easy as pie to set up. Looks like she was wrong."

Four cats sat at their feet looking glum after the kibble incident. Odelia explained to them what Gran had told her about the Franklin Cooper factory being shut down by the FDA three years ago. And even though it mitigated what they considered a gross negligence of her duties as a pet parent, they still continued to look glum over the loss of their favorite kibble. She now remembered she had bought a lot of the stuff back then, and now wondered if that was the reason it had been so cheap: because the factory had been closed down.

So maybe she had been feeding the cats poisoned cat kibble for a while. The thought made her feel sick. But since the cats seemed to be in excellent health, maybe it had all been one big hullabaloo over nothing, as sometimes happened with these so-called food scandals.

At least all of the Franklin Cooper kibble was gone now, so that put her mind at ease. And as she picked up Grace and told Chase that dinner was at her parents' place, she swept out the door.

CHAPTER 11

Freddie had been nervous about venturing out again after bumping into the same woman twice in one day. And since he really wanted to take a closer look at that old house he'd seen, he decided to wait until after dark to do it. When his mom asked where he was going, he simply said, "Out." And since they had that kind of relationship, she didn't ask any more.

He could have told her that he was looking at places to buy, and she would have been overjoyed, while still trying to hide the fact and assuring him that she and Dad didn't want him out of the house—no way!

He drove his old car along streets that were anything but deserted. In fact, it almost looked as if all of Hampton Cove had had the same idea he'd had and had decided to come out of their houses in droves. Maybe it was the heat. Now that the sun was finally tucked in for the night and the temperatures were dropping to a more agreeable level, people felt it was finally safe to venture outside, and so they took full use of the fact.

At a leisurely pace, he steered his vehicle in the direction of the house he'd seen, looked around for a sign of the woman whose bumper he'd dented before accidentally knocking her out, and when he saw there was not a single sign of her, got out of the car and glanced up at the house. Backlit by a full moon, it looked more eerie than ever and wouldn't have looked bad featured in a horror movie. But since he was a horror movie fanatic, he didn't mind. In fact, it was part of its appeal as far as he was concerned.

He passed through the ramshackle little gate that hung crooked on its ancient hinges, crossed the patch of derelict jungle that had once been the front yard, and up the few steps that led to the front door. The door had a little window in it that he now tried to peek through at the space beyond. All in all, he got the impression that once upon a time, this must have been a very fine house and must have set its owners back a pretty penny.

Now, though, it didn't look like much, except the dwelling of the lord of the underworld and his denizens. But since that didn't deter him in the slightest, he decided to try the front door so he could take a look around. When the door didn't yield to the pressure applied to it, he circled around and approached the house from the back. And he stood looking up at the back facade wondering if a simple paint job and a couple of new roof tiles wouldn't do the job of returning the place to its former glory when he suddenly saw a man and a woman carrying a body out of a van parked on the street.

And if he wasn't mistaken, it was the same woman who'd given him such grief that morning!

As he stood staring at the duo, for a moment, nothing stirred. Then all of a sudden, the woman must have sensed that someone was watching her, for she turned her head, and as she did, their eyes locked. She seemed to freeze where she stood, and as the man also looked in his direction, he let rip a cry of shock and horror and even went so far as to drop the body. The sheet with which they had covered it fell away, and he now saw that it was a man with something lodged in his head. And if he wasn't mistaken, it was a toy dragon.

The sight was so unusual that a guffaw escaped his throat, before covering his mouth with his hand and ducking down and out of sight. Of course, it was far too late for that, for he had already been seen. And as he decided to make a run for it and escape with his life, a heavy hand suddenly descended on his shoulder, and when he looked up, he saw that it was her, and this time she wasn't going to let him incapacitate her with a nice right hook to her chin—though truth be told he wouldn't be able to replicate that freak incident even if he tried.

"You!" she said as she fixed him with a particularly unfriendly look. She then turned to the other man. "This is the guy I was telling you about."

"Oh, so this is the guy who knocked you out, is it?"

"That's right. Knocked me out and fled the scene of the accident he caused."

"There was no accident," he said. "And I didn't flee the scene."

"You hit my car with your car."

"No, I didn't."

She rolled her eyes. "Next thing you're going to tell me you didn't knock me out."

"I didn't knock you out."

"So why did I wake up with a bruise the size of a pancake on my face?"

He shrugged. "How should I know? Maybe you dreamt the whole thing?"

"I didn't dream the whole thing!" she cried, raising her voice, as seemed to be her habit.

"Look, I didn't see anything, if that's what you're worried

about," he said, gesturing with his head to the dead man, who still lay there on the ground, ready for whatever they were planning to do with him.

For a moment, the two murderers didn't speak, then the man piped up, "It's not what it looks like."

"It never is," he said generously. "So can I go now?"

"No," said the woman coldly.

"I mean, I didn't see nothing. No dead body. No..." He glanced over and winced as he saw that toy. "No dragon sticking out of its head."

"It was an accident," the man said.

"He fell and hit his head on a toy dragon?"

"Something like that." He gave him a nervous look. "Look, we can make a deal, can't we?"

"Absolutely," he assured the killer. "What deal did you have in mind, exactly?"

"We'll let you go if you promise not to call the police."

"Deal," he said immediately, and stuck out his hand to shake on it.

"Not so fast," said the woman. She leaned in dangerously. "You knocked me out, and then you fled the scene of the crime."

"No, I didn't," he said, but was starting to feel that his denial wasn't making a big impression. Which it wouldn't, since this woman was some kind of psychopath. And since he didn't feel like being her next victim, he decided to make a run for it. He didn't get very far, for he'd only run as far as the back door of the house he'd planned to visit when he tripped and fell, and when he looked back, he saw that the woman was the one who had tripped him up. She now pushed a knee into his right kidney and wrenched his arm back.

"Ouch," he said, since it really hurt.

"You're coming with us," she breathed.

"Oh, that sounds great," he said. "Where are we going? Is it somewhere nice?"

"Less talk, more cooperation," she growled, and yanked him to his feet.

"Where are we taking him?" asked the other guy.

"Inside," she said.

"But... I mean, we can't..."

She shut him up with a single look. "Yes, we can," she said emphatically.

And that, as far as he was concerned, probably sealed his fate. He glanced up at his dream house—which quite possibly appealed to no one else but him—and figured he'd never get to live there. These two were going to murder him with that dragon and dump his body. But as luck would have it, just then a car passed, and as he broke free from the hold the woman had on him, he threw himself on top of that car. With his face plastered against the windshield, he screamed, "Help me! They want to murder me! Help me please!"

The car stopped so abruptly that he rolled off the hood and fell to the ground. But when he looked up, he saw the woman standing over him, accompanied by the people in the car, who didn't look all that friendly, he had to say, or predisposed to saving his life! She grinned widely and said, "Meet my husband, bozo. He's going to help me take care of you once and for all!"

CHAPTER 12

It didn't take us long to convince Gran to assist us in retrieving the kibble that Odelia had so unadvisedly thrown on the compost heap. I just hoped it would still be salvageable. That compost heap is a source of pride to Tex but a source of concern to the rest of us, since it mostly contains a lot of rotting and decaying stuff, which attracts the bug element. And since bugs also like to eat, I could only imagine what would happen to our precious kibble if it remained on that compost for too long.

"Okay, I'll do it," said Gran after we had explained the situation to her. "But on one condition."

"And what's that?" I asked.

"That the four of you will accompany me on my patrols from now on."

We had known this was coming, of course, and decided to drive a hard bargain. "One night," said Brutus.

"Seven," Gran threw back.

"Three," said Harriet.

"Five!"

"Two," said Dooley.

Gran laughed. "You obviously don't know anything about the art of the bargain, Dooley. You can't go back on your position."

"Four," said Harriet.

"Deal," said Gran and held out her hand, which Harriet shook with a grave look on her face, as if it was a terrible hardship to give in. Truth be told, sometimes these patrols get a little tedious, but more often than not they're also fun, especially when something exciting happens. The problem was that we'd have to forego our cat choir sessions, which especially for Harriet is tough, as she always looks forward to these rehearsals.

"Okay, so let's talk kibble," said Gran.

Fifi, who had also joined us in the backyard, since it had been her idea in the first place, said, "That's what I've been meaning to ask. What's wrong with the kibble, Gran?"

"The thing is, I'm not sure," said Gran truthfully. "As I explained to Odelia and Tex, there was a huge scandal back in the day, but since the FDA would never disclose what the problem was, and obviously the Coopers didn't want to say either, we never got to find out. So for all we know, there could be some contamination going on."

"I never noticed anything off about that kibble," said Brutus. "And I may be considered an expert on kibble. I eat the stuff all the time, you see."

"I never tasted anything out of the ordinary about that kibble either," I said. On the contrary. The best-tasting kibble ever made available to cat-kind, in my personal opinion.

"Okay, so let's just go and save that kibble, shall we?" said Gran. "And then you can decide whether there's something wrong with it or not. But if you get constipation or diarrhea or if you start seeing weird things, don't come crying to me when we have to take you to see Vena, all right?"

"Fine," I said, though the prospect of having to pay a visit to the family vet terrified me to no end, for obvious reasons, such as there are: her penchant for sticking needles into us at the slightest provocation!

"We can't do this now," said Gran. "Since Odelia won't like it, and nor will Marge. So we'll have to wait until everyone is fast asleep. So this is what we'll do. We'll meet in the backyard after midnight. By that time, they should all be asleep. And then immediately after, we'll go on our first patrol together."

"Is this new guy going to join in as well?" I asked, for I'd heard some noise about a new recruit.

"Yes, he will," said Gran, though judging from the way her face twitched, it was clear that she wasn't fully in favor of this man joining her precious neighborhood watch. But then to keep any of these organizations alive, it's sometimes necessary to attract new blood. "But if he makes a nuisance of himself, and I just know he will, he's out on his ear." Then she softened. "Scarlett thinks he'll behave, though, so there's that. And since she knows this guy better than I do, maybe I should reserve judgment until we've ascertained whether he'll be a boon or a drag."

And so it was arranged: we'd wait until all of our humans were fast asleep, and then Operation Save Kibble would commence. Hopefully, by then, there would still be something left of that much-treasured and much-beloved Franklin Cooper!

Gran returned indoors to watch some television, and the five of us talked turkey.

"What are we going to do with the kibble once we save it?" asked Harriet. "I mean, we can't keep it lying around the house. Odelia will notice, and the moment she does, she will throw it out again. So we have to find a safe place to store it."

"We could store it in the garden house?" Brutus

suggested. "Tex doesn't go in there a lot these days, and Marge never goes there, and neither does Odelia."

"It's a possibility," Harriet accepted. "But isn't it dangerous to keep food in there? It will attract vermin, and they might eat the whole stash."

"She's right," I said. "That kibble will be gone in a heartbeat if we put it in the shed."

"But then where?" asked Harriet. She glanced at Fifi, who she had come to accept as a master strategist by now. "What do you think, Fifi? Any bright ideas?"

Fifi had been thinking hard, as evidenced by the frown that marred her furry features. "The only thing I would suggest is that you store it at my place. In the pantry, mixed in with the rest of the kibble. Kurt keeps bags and bags of my kibble in there—he's a hoarder of the stuff. And so a couple of bags more or less won't be noticeable. And then any time you want to snack on that wonderful Franklin Cooper, you simply tell me, and I'll sneak you into the house."

It seemed like a good idea. Kurt was the only one not aware of Odelia's prejudice against anything to do with that particular brand name. So if he accidentally came upon a bag of the stuff, he wouldn't feel the sudden urge to throw it out. He'd simply figure it belonged to Fifi and would go about his way, thus preserving the stuff for us.

"A great idea," said Brutus, heaping praise where praise was due. "So Gran will have to sneak into Kurt's kitchen."

"Pantry," Fifi amended.

"Gran will sneak into your pantry and place the kibble amongst your stash. That way, no one will ever be any the wiser that we managed to preserve the best kibble in the world for posterity."

"You're not going to eat it?" asked Fifi, much surprised.

"Well, we haven't actually decided what we're going to do

with it," said Brutus, glancing at the rest of us. "So what do you think, guys? As you may remember, the options are sending it to a lab to have it reverse-engineered and then mass-produced so we'll have Franklin Cooper for the rest of our lives. Or we could also eat it and be done with it. Forget that it ever existed."

I made a face. "It's going to be hard to forget that Franklin Cooper ever existed," I said.

"I hear you, Max," said my friend. "And I feel exactly the same way."

"What's the third option?" asked Harriet. "I forget."

"Sell it to the highest bidder," said Brutus. "Since it's very likely that this is the last Franklin Cooper in the world, and there will be others who crave it even more than we do and want to pay through the nose for the privilege of owning even a single pellet of the stuff."

We all thought about these options for a moment. And even though I was sorely tempted to simply eat everything, I knew that wasn't the way forward-thinking cats acted.

"I say we send half of it to the lab," said Dooley. "And we sell the rest. The money we make from the sale will pay for the lab," he explained, "and make sure we'll have Franklin Cooper forever and ever."

We all stared at him with surprise. It was the smartest thing I'd ever heard anyone say. "Dooley, that's brilliant!" said Harriet. "That way we have the three options all in one perfect solution!"

"Absolute genius," Brutus grunted approvingly.

"I like it," said Fifi. "A very elegant solution, Dooley."

Dooley now stared at me, the only one who hadn't commented.

"What do you think, Max?" he asked eagerly.

"Well, if we can rope Gran into giving us another helping hand, I think your solution is the best one possible. So I say let's go for it, buddy. And congratulations for coming up with this."

He smiled widely, fully satisfied that he had given of his best. "Thanks, Max. Coming from you, that's high praise indeed." And so we all slapped our friend on the back, causing him to giggle happily. "Now all we have to do is save that kibble from Tex's compost heap, and we're back in business!"

CHAPTER 13

I was so happy that the heat had finally subsided, and that I could breathe again, that I felt fully alive that night. The fact that we were about to go on a very daring but also exciting mission may have had something to do with that, of course. I wanted to save that kibble and was prepared to sit in Gran's car for a few nights to do it, if that was what it took. In fact, I counted the minutes until the clock finally indicated that midnight had arrived, and we could join Gran on this most important adventure.

I had a feeling that Odelia suspected that we were up to something, for even as the four of us lay on the couch and watched a movie together as a family, she kept darting curious looks in my direction and asking if I was truly all right. Apparently, Dooley's words that I had been close to my own expiration date had given her quite a fright.

"I'm fine," I said breezily. "Fine as a fiddle." And if she kept that fan running and also that portable AC system that Chase had finally managed to start up, with a little help from his father-in-law, I might even survive the next couple of days, which the weather people had promised would be 'hotter than a furnace in hell!' They do have a way with words, these weather mavens.

"I like this air conditioner," said Chase as he nodded approvingly. "Though we have to keep it away from Grace, of course," he hastened to add. "Make sure she doesn't catch a cold."

"I won't catch a cold, Daddy," the little girl said. "You make sure you don't catch a cold, with that air conditioner at full blast at your office."

Uncle Alec had splurged and had outfitted the police station with these same air conditioners, making sure that our local constabulary kept a cool head at all times. It wouldn't do for the criminal underbelly of our town to get ideas above their station, simply because the police were slowly expiring from the heat, and their response times had turned sluggish as a consequence.

Though truth be told, I couldn't imagine the criminals being all that active either, since they might be bad, but they were still human and must suffer from the heat as much or even more than their law-abiding counterparts, who didn't have to crawl through windows or scale walls and climb on top of roofs to provide for their families through ill-gotten means.

Finally, the movie ended—it was one of those soapy romance stories that I dislike so much but that Odelia loves, and Chase tolerates. Grace was being put to bed, something she doesn't like, since she wants to stay up as long as her mom and dad do. And after the little girl had been relegated to her cot, our humans decided to stay up a little longer, consume a glass of wine, and start watching a Netflix rom-com series. I could have told them that it would all end well, and that the couple would find each other in the end, but they probably wouldn't have believed me. I had a feeling that Chase would have preferred to watch some thriller or action show where people shoot other people a lot, and in the end everyone is dead except the hero, but clearly Odelia wasn't in the mood for that kind of thing.

The four of us exchanged concerned glances when the clock drew nearer and nearer to our go-time, and still our humans didn't stir. Didn't they have work to go to tomorrow? But then I guess this binge-watchable stuff is so addictive it's hard to wrestle yourself away from it. Finally, the episode ended with the kiss, and we all breathed a sigh of relief. Odelia seemed to be in a frisky mood, in spite of the fact that it was a weeknight, and the upshot was that she and Chase hurriedly disappeared upstairs.

"This is it, you guys," said Harriet. "Time to get this mission on the road!"

And so it was. We hurried out through the pet flap and into the backyard next door to meet Gran. The old lady sat on the back porch and seemed a little annoyed. "What took you so long? I've been waiting for hours!"

"Impossible," I said. "The clock has just struck midnight ten minutes ago."

"Be that as it may, Tex and Marge have gone to bed at eleven, and I've been bored out of my skull waiting for you guys to show up," she grumbled as she slipped off the swing and joined us in the backyard. She was dressed in black from head to foot: black sweater, black sweatpants, and even black tennis shoes. Clearly, she had taken her precautions and was ready for this mission to go well. "I've got a bag, and I've got a scoop," she announced, showing us the tools of the kibble-stealing trade with a proud smile. "So let's do this!"

We all moved stealthily in the direction of Tex's big compost heap, located behind his garden house, and when Gran shone a light on the heap, we found to our surprise that of the kibble, there was not a single trace.

"But... where is it?" asked Harriet.

"I don't understand," said Gran. "I thought you said that Tex had deposited it here?"

"He did," I said. "So it must be here somewhere."

For a few moments, Gran rooted around in search of our kibble, and when she couldn't find it, scratched her scalp in abject bewilderment. "I don't get it. Where is that stuff?"

And then I saw it: a small troop of ants was hoisting up what looked like the last piece of kibble and transporting it in the direction of the fence.

"Hey!" I said. "What do you think you're doing!"

The leader of the ants halted the forward progression of the regiment and gave me a curious look. "Oh, it's you again," he said, and I now recognized him as Lucian. "Max, is it?"

"That's right. What are you doing with our kibble?"

"Your kibble? I don't see your name written on it," said the annoying ant leader.

"Did you take all of it?" I asked.

"All of it," he confirmed. "And a nice big haul it was, too. Our queen will be very happy."

"You took all of our kibble!" I cried.

"Like I said, it didn't have your name on it, so as far as I'm concerned, it's finders keepers. See you, Max. Take care." And with these words, he instructed his small troupe to move out with these few remaining pieces of kibble—the last of their kind.

"What's going on?" asked Gran.

"The ants took the kibble," I said. "They're just carting off the last few nuggets."

"They've taken them to their queen," said Dooley. "She must be one hungry queen, though, for there were three bags of kibble on this compost heap and now they're all gone."

"Queens are always hungry," said Harriet, and she should know, since she was a queen herself, of course. "It's because they have to give birth to a full colony of ants."

"But but but," Brutus sputtered. "This can't be happening. Our kibble, you guys. Gone! All of it!"

"Maybe we can negotiate its return?" Harriet suggested. She gave me a slight shove. "You do it, Max. This Lucian seems to like you."

"He doesn't," I said. "In fact, I get the impression that he doesn't like any of us."

"Probably because we're all in the market for the same type of food," said Harriet. She steeled herself. "Okay, so let me give it a shot." And so she approached the small column of ants, now moving up the fence, preparatory to going over and disappearing forever. "You guys?" she said. "Just a moment, will you?"

"What is it now, cat?" said Lucian, their fearless leader—or maybe he was a general. As indicated I'm not all that well-versed in ant colony terminology.

"Could you perhaps leave us a few pellets? That way we can have them analyzed in a lab and maybe reproduced. They're our favorite, you see. And we want to save them."

"Too late," said Lucian. "These have all been earmarked for our queen. Adios, cat."

"But you can't do this," she said. "You can't take everything and leave nothing for us!"

"And yet we just did," said the ant—small in stature but big in sheer brass.

"Can't we share?" Harriet tried again. "Just a few of those nuggets? You have plenty, don't you?"

"Have you seen the size of our colony?" asked Lucian. "Then you'd know that's a silly question, cat. In fact, this is just a drop in the bucket for us. So if you know of a place where they've got more of this stuff, please let me know, will you? All hail to the queen."

"All hail to the queen!" his fellow ants bellowed, and with this, they went up and over the fence and were gone, taking the last few pieces of Franklin Cooper on the planet along with them.

We were sad to see them go, but what could we do? Ants are tricky creatures. If you try to thwart them, they might bite—and an ant bite is nothing to sneer at. It stings! And since there are so many of them, when they do attack, you're in for a pretty rough ride.

"So that's it?" said Gran. "You're giving up? Just like that?"

"They're ants, Gran," said Harriet. "There's probably billions of them and only four of us."

"Yeah, if they attack us in our sleep, we'll be nothing but a gnawed-off skeleton by the time they're through," said Brutus. "So better not to engage them in a fight that we can't possibly win."

"Okay, fine," said Gran. "So let's go."

We all stared at her. "Go where?"

"On my patrol, of course. You did promise me four nights."

"But… that was before we knew that our kibble was going to get stolen by the ants," I said.

"A deal is a deal," said the old lady. "So let's go. Scarlett is waiting, and also the new guy. And we don't want to make a bad first impression. The reputation of the watch depends on it. So chop chop!"

And so we moved out, single file, not unlike Lucian's troupe. Though with a lot less excitement about the night that we had ahead of us. But coming upon the shock of seeing our kibble being carried away on the backs of a column of ants, sitting in a car with Gran for a couple of hours was the least of our concerns. Without Franklin Cooper's Premium Pet Food, life suddenly seemed meaningless.

Stretching out in front of us was a long desert of sheer tedium and hopelessness!

CHAPTER 14

Freddie didn't feel as if his transgressions deserved such a harsh rebuke. Even when judged in a regular court of law, he would never have risked the death penalty for accidentally knocking out a woman. Okay, so he had scratched her car, but to sentence him to death over such a trifle seemed excessive by any standards. Though he would soon find out there was at least one silver lining to his predicament: he was about to set foot inside the house he had earmarked for his own. He would have preferred to see it with a real estate agent, who would have pointed out the pros and cons of the dilapidated old building. Instead, he was being marched in through the back door and then down a rickety flight of stairs into the cellar, to be locked up in a dank old room, the door slammed in his face.

"Hey!" he said, rattling the handle. "Let me out of here!"

But of course there was no response. Which is when he decided to start looking for a way out. But try as he might, he couldn't find one. The room had no windows, bar a very small one that he couldn't possibly squeeze through. Only the one door, and no other means of escape. And so, in the end, he simply sank down on a bed that had been placed in a corner of the room. As he looked around, he wondered what the room might have been used for. If he would have ventured a guess, he would have said it looked very much like a prison cell, with the small bed with the ratty mattress and the single table with a single chair and the small wardrobe. He got up to inspect the wardrobe but found it empty, as he should have expected. And as he returned to the bed, he hoped they wouldn't keep him in there too long. Then again, maybe what he should be hoping for was to escape from this place with his life.

* * *

REBEKKA PACED the floor of the upstairs living room, which, like the rest of the house, had seen better days. "I still say we should get rid of him," she argued. She darted a glance in the direction of the other room, where the toy maker sat awaiting her return. "Probably we should get rid of that guy as well."

"But I thought he killed that guy?" asked her husband.

"Of course he did, but that doesn't mean he won't regret his actions sooner or later and spill the beans to the cops. And since I'm involved now up to my eyeballs, that means we're better off without him." She gave her hubby of fourteen years a pleading look. "Please make them both go away, Dirk. I simply can't deal with it, on top of everything else."

"Why did you bring him here in the first place?"

She shrugged. "I figured he'd make a good recruit. You know we're always looking for new people. And you should have seen him handling that toy dragon. One strike and it was game over."

"It's not my place to criticize your decisions, baby," said her husband carefully, "but to be honest he doesn't strike me as the kind of asset we can use. That hit was just a lucky strike. A one-time thing that he deeply regrets now. And it would greatly surprise me that a toy store owner would be interested in launching a career in organized crime." He held up his hands. "Just my personal opinion."

He was right, she saw that now. To be honest she hadn't been thinking straight. When that guy waved that gun in her face, she should simply have gone along with him and then, when she got the chance, overpowered him, not suggest she assist him in covering up his crime. A trip to the cops and it would have been over. But no, she had to go and consider hiring Mr. Bennett for the family business. And on top of that, suggest that they use their GHQ to store the body for the time being. Stupid stupid stupid!

"The thing is, we can't go around killing people left and right," said Dirk. Very sensibly, she thought, even if a little annoying and disappointing. "Every time we get rid of someone, it creates a big risk. And we don't need that. Definitely not when we're already facing a shit storm of epic proportions."

He was right, of course. What with her dad acting all weird lately, they should probably take it easy and maybe even lay low for a while. "Look, I didn't ask for this guy to murder a man right in front of me, or for this other fella to catch us shifting a dead body. It happened, and now we have to deal with it. So the best thing would be to..." She flapped her arms. "Well, to make them all go away!"

Dirk nodded thoughtfully as he rubbed his chin. "Okay, here's what we'll do. For the moment, we're not going to make them go away—at least not permanently. We're simply going to keep them on ice. I'll get an expert in, and he'll take care of everything. How about that?"

"What expert?" she asked suspiciously. The last 'expert' they had asked to take care of a similar problem for them had made a big mess of things. In the end, they'd had to take care of the expert, and the problem he was supposed to handle.

"Buddy Catt," said Dirk, and immediately she relaxed.

"I didn't know Buddy was still active," she said.

"Oh, no, he is. Not as active as he used to be, maybe. More selective with the kind of work he accepts, but he's still a valuable and popular operator." He approached and took her in his arms. She tilted her face up to his, and they shared a kiss. "So that's agreed?"

"Yes," she said, well pleased. If Buddy was on the case, she could relax. He always did a great job, as they all knew from past experience. "With Buddy on the case, I know everything will be fine."

"Good," he said. "He costs a pretty penny, but we both know he's worth it. So I'll bring him in, and you can focus on the rest. Do you think you can handle that?"

She nodded fervently. "I *was* handling it, only this…" She waved in the general direction of the floor. "This *clown* had to go and make a nuisance of himself."

He put two hands on her shoulders. "Hey. It's all right, sweetie. Dirk is handling it. Okay?"

"Okay," she said, and felt the tension drain from her neck and shoulders. "Thanks, babe."

"Don't mention it. Now about your dad…"

She groaned. "Let's not go there."

"We have to. What are we going to do about your old man?"

And as they discussed the ways and means of making sure that her dad was well taken care of, suddenly Felix Bennett's face appeared in the door. "Sorry to interrupt, but I'd like to go home now."

She exchanged a look with her husband, and as he gave her an almost imperceptible nod, she moved over to the toy store owner and gave the man a reassuring smile. "Absolutely," she assured him. "We'll take you home soon. In the meantime, could you wait for us in there? We won't be long, I promise." And as she escorted him in the direction of one of the empty rooms, she waited until he was inside and then closed and locked the door. He'd be all right in there until Buddy would arrive to get rid of him.

Moments later she was back in the old living room, discussing with her husband what to do about her dad. He might be a pain in the behind, but he was still her father, and she loved him. So whatever they did, they should do it with the respect he deserved as the head of the family—now pretty much retired.

"A nursing home would be best," Dirk suggested. And when she started to protest, he stressed, "Babe, you know he hasn't been himself lately. And with your mom in hospital, we need to do something."

He probably had a point. Ever since her mom had a stroke and ended up in intensive care, her dad had been living alone, and, to be honest, he wasn't in a fit state to be alone anymore. So finally she agreed. "Okay, let's find him a nice home he can go to. He won't like it, but that's too bad."

"It's for his own good," said Dirk as he rubbed her back. "And I'm sure deep inside he knows that."

Until a couple of days ago, she had still harbored high hopes that her mother would recover and be ready to go home soon. But the doctor at the hospital had told them in no uncertain terms that Mom might never be the same again, and that she couldn't possibly go home—not unless someone was there to take care of her. And with Dad in the state he was in, that wasn't a possibility. And since both Dirk and she led pretty busy lives, they couldn't take care of her parents either. So all that was left was to make arrangements that they could go to some nice nursing home where they could live out their old age in as comfortable and pleasant surroundings as possible. Her brothers wouldn't agree, but that couldn't be helped. They were idiots anyway. At least one member of the family had both the brains and the courage to make these tough decisions. Though if it wasn't for Dirk, she didn't know what she would have done. And so she stood on her tiptoes and planted a kiss on his lips.

"Thanks," she whispered.

"For what?"

"For always being there," she said. "And for being the voice of reason."

He gave her that killer smile that always melted her heart. "No sweat, babe."

Just then, one of her brothers arrived, and she took a deep breath. "Time to get to work!"

"No rest for the wicked," he agreed with a grin.

And she turned to face her brother and break the bad news to him that their mom and dad would soon go and live in a nursing home. As expected, Daavid didn't take the news too well.

CHAPTER 15

Franklin Cooper. The name had been on all of our minds for what felt like days now, though it had only been since we made the startling discovery that a few bags of the phenomenal stuff still remained. And so even though we should have been working hard to thwart crime in Hampton Cove by riding in the back of Gran's car, all we could think of was those infernal ants, whose queen was at that very moment stuffing herself with our kibble!

The new guy, as Gran kept calling him, turned out to be a nice gentleman who answered to the name Cliff Puckering. He was a kindly old man who was sick and tired that his street had been turned into a haven for hooligans, drug dealers and annoying little punks, as he referred to them, and wished to do something about it, "Since the police don't seem to be able or willing to."

"I know how you feel," Gran assured him as she steered the car to the neighborhood in question. "I've often told my son that he should be more proactive, but he claims he doesn't have the manpower."

"Alec does the best he can," said Scarlett, who's a big fan

of Uncle Alec. "And it's true that he simply doesn't have enough officers to patrol the streets and keep us all safe twenty-four-seven."

"Which is where we come in," her friend said with a nod. She glanced in the rear-view mirror. "So what do you suggest we do, Cliff?"

"Well, for starters, we could patrol the street where all of this mayhem is happening," the pensioner suggested. "That should scare them off, don't you think?"

Gran and Scarlett shared an amused smile. "No, it won't. These kinds of people aren't easily scared off," said Scarlett. "To do that, you should probably descend on them en masse and make sure to throw every single last one of them in prison and let them simmer for a while."

"Bring them before a judge," Gran confirmed. "Who won't be lenient on them."

"But how are we going to do that?" said Cliff, who looked disappointed. "We can't arrest them, can we?"

"Well, we could try," said Scarlett. "But they'd probably run rings around us."

"I'm not exactly a hero at this kind of stuff," said Gran. "I don't even have a black belt. Unless you're an expert at martial arts?" she suggested cheekily.

Cliff had to admit that he didn't have a black belt in any arts, and certainly not of the martial kind. "So I guess that's it? We simply declare defeat? Let the bad guys win?"

"We didn't say that," said Scarlett as she turned to face their new recruit. "We have to catch them in the act, Cliff."

"And how do we do that?" he asked.

"Let's first wait and see what we're dealing with here," Gran suggested, and parked the car at the top of the street, doused her lights, and settled down to take in the scene.

As Cliff had promised, the scene wasn't pretty. About a dozen kids on motorcycles and bikes raced up and down the street, from time to time knocking off a side mirror here or hitting a flowerpot there and generally not creating a pleasant environment for the people living on the street. And as we watched on, two kids stood nearby, and it was obvious they weren't up to any good. One of them handed something in a little plastic baggie to the other, who handed over a wad of cash.

"Drug dealing!" said Cliff. "Brazen as can be! I told Mindy, but she wouldn't buy it!"

"*He's* buying it," said Brutus, referring to the kid who went off on his bike with the plastic baggie on his person. "Though I wonder what it is exactly that he's buying."

"Drugs, of course," said Harriet. "Isn't it always drugs that these kids are into?"

Gran had taken a couple of pictures of the transaction, and now studied them on her phone. "Looks like some kind of pills," she announced. "Little brown ones. I don't think I've ever seen them before." She handed her phone to her friend. "Here. Take a look."

"Odd," said Scarlett as she zoomed in on the pills. "They almost look like... diet pills."

Gran smiled. "And how would you know what diet pills look like?" But when Scarlett gave her an 'Are you kidding me' look, she amended her question. "Oh, of course. I should have known. What are they called again? Olympic?"

"Ozempic," said Scarlett. "And I stopped taking them, as you well know. And besides, they're not brown but white. So these are definitely not Ozempic. They're the organic kind."

"What would kids need diet pills for?" asked Cliff. A good question, and one to which none of us had the answer.

More bike racing commenced, and when one of the kids threw a couple of firecrackers underneath one of the cars parked in front of us and they exploded with a loud bang and a lot of smoke, Gran said, "Okay, enough is enough. I'm calling it in."

And so she took out her phone and dialed her son's number. "Alec? Sorry to wake you, but Scarlett and Cliff and I are parked on Gillard Street and it's pandemonium out here. Kids dealing drugs, throwing bombs under parked cars, and creating a big mess. Can you send a couple of your officers and make a couple of arrests, please? Cliff's neighbors will be very grateful. Thank you." And as she disconnected, she caught Cliff's odd look. "Oh, didn't I tell you? My son is chief of police. He'll send a squad car to take a look."

She looked awfully proud as she spoke these words, and judging from Cliff's look of awe, he was extremely appreciative of her ready response to his most urgent request.

"Thank you, Vesta," he said brokenly. "And I apologize once again for the trouble I caused at the senior center that time."

She waved a deprecating hand. "Water under the bridge," she assured him. "I was as much to blame as you. I should never have thrown that cactus at your head."

"And I should never have called you a stupid woman," he said ruefully.

"Okay, so maybe let's get out of here?" Scarlett suggested. "We don't want to be here when the shit hits the fan, do we?"

And so Gran started up the car, and as she emerged from the parking spot, one of the kids caught sight of us, and he must have become aware that his drug-dealing ways had been witnessed, for he launched himself in our direction on his motorcycle, and the determined look on his face told me that he wasn't going to let us drive away so easily.

"We're being followed, Gran!" I told our human urgently.

Gran looked back, and when she saw the kid coming, plunked her foot down on the accelerator. The motorbike sped up behind us and was on our bumper now. Which is when Gran suddenly stomped her foot on the brake. The car skidded to a halt, and the motorcycle, unable to respond with the same alacrity, hit us in the rear, went skidding over the car, and landed right in front of us. The kid looked a little worse for wear as he crawled to his feet. And as Gran deftly circumvented him, she gave him a wave.

"See you around!" she yelled, and then was off at a rapid clip. "Better call an ambulance," she told Scarlett, "to go with those squad cars."

"Where did you learn to drive like that?" asked Cliff.

"Who says I ever learned how to drive?" asked Gran. And as we raced away from the scene, three police cars passed us by, going in the other direction.

"That was quick service," said Cliff with admiration. "And to think that I must have called them at least a dozen times, and they never sent any squad car round."

"It pays to have a son who works for the police," said Gran.

"And even more when he hates to disappoint his mother," Scarlett added.

Though I could have told her it wasn't fear of disappointment that mostly prompted Uncle Alec to do as Gran told him, but fear of the retribution if he didn't. Gran has a tendency to follow her own instincts, and more often than not, these tend to clash with the law, strictly speaking.

CHAPTER 16

Alec plunked his head back down on the pillow and groaned audibly.

"What's wrong, honey?" asked his wife sleepily. "Who was that?"

"Do you have to ask? My mother, of course."

"What's she up to now?"

"Oh, something about some punks making a nuisance of themselves. Same thing every night, only now she seems to have gotten it into her head that she needs to intervene."

Charlene set up in bed. "You should tell her to be careful," she said. "These kids might be a nuisance, but some of them are actually hardened criminals and might come after her."

"Oh, I know," said Alec with a wistful look on his face. But when Charlene eyed him sternly, he quickly wiped it off his face. "I will tell her," he said. "But you know what my mother is like. She never listens to anything I tell her, so it won't do much good."

"Is this the Gillard Street youth gang?" asked Charlene, and when Alec nodded, she frowned. "I've been meaning to talk to you about that. Rumor has it they're turning into a real menace. At first, it was just some mischief and some minor vandalism, but now they're also into dealing drugs. Maybe you should set up a task force to handle the situation."

"I will, I will," he promised. "As long as my mother doesn't interfere, we should be able to get a handle on the situation soon... ish." It was true that he was seriously understaffed to deal with these kinds of contingencies, but it was also true that the people living on that block had complained incessantly about these kids, who were starting to really annoy the heck out of the police chief. He couldn't wait to root out their nonsense—if all parties agreed to cooperate.

"Who's behind these drugs?" asked Charlene. "Who's their supplier?"

Alec shrugged. "Who knows? That's what the task force will have to determine."

She nodded, then settled down between the sheets again. "Keep me informed, will you?"

"Of course," he promised, and as he listened to his wife's deep and even breathing, he hoped his mother would stay out of this whole mess. Every time she got involved in something, it only led to a lot of trouble. And since these people didn't mess around, it might put her life in jeopardy as well— which was the last thing they needed. He'd never hear the end of it.

* * *

DOOLEY HAD BEEN nervous from the moment they set out on this patrol. First of all, he was still worried about his friend Max's health. He may look fine now, but he hadn't forgotten that only a few hours previously he had been lying on that basement floor, practically comatose. Even if Max now put on a brave face, he had the distinct impression his friend still wasn't feeling A-okay but was acting like he was so as not to disappoint any of them. That was the kind of cat Max was: always putting the others first and himself and his well-being last.

But Dooley wasn't going to let him. If anything, he felt that his friend should be resting now to get his strength back. This heat wave might still persist for another couple of days, and so it behooved them to keep a close eye on Max and make sure he was all right.

"Have you drunk enough water?" he asked now.

"Yes, Dooley, I have," Max assured him.

"Have you eaten? Even though you may not be hungry, on account of the heat, you should still eat," he told his friend.

"I have eaten," Max said.

"So how are you feeling?" he asked, as he studied his friend closely.

"I'm feeling perfectly fine," said Max, starting to sound a little annoyed at his barrage of questions. "And now will you please let me focus on this patrol? There may be more people up to no good, and it's our job to locate them and to alert Gran when we do."

"Forget about the bad people," he advised. "You should be thinking about yourself now, Max. You haven't been feeling too good, and you should take it easy."

"I *am* taking it easy!" he assured him. "I'm resting peacefully in the back of a car, being chauffeured around. How much more easy can I take it?"

"But you're not resting, are you? To be truly resting you should be home right now, on the foot of Odelia's bed, getting a little shut-eye while you still can. Tomorrow promises to be another scorcher, and you know you don't respond well to the heat."

Max sighed. "Can we please simply focus on the patrol? I'm fine!" he added when Dooley brought his face close to

Max's and studied the whites of his eyes for any sign of fatigue.

"Dooley is right, Max," said Harriet. "You shouldn't be out on patrol with us. You should be at home taking it easy. Maybe even get a massage or something." She held up her nails. "Or you could join me at the pet salon tomorrow morning. It's always nice and cool in there, and being pampered like that will make you feel so relaxed you'll forget all about this silly heatwave."

"I don't want to go to the pet salon," said Max, starting to sound a little rattled. "I'm fine, I'm telling you."

"You don't look fine, Max," said Brutus, adding his own voice to the choir. "I hope you don't mind me saying this, but you look sick. And if I were you, I'd ask Odelia to take me to see Vena tomorrow. You may be suffering from some heart condition. It's very taxing on the heart, you know, this heat. And we both know that you're not in good health. Overweight," he added.

"I'm not overweight!" Max cried. "And will you please leave me alone. I'm fine, I'm telling you!"

Cliff, who was sitting next to them in the back seat, had been shuffling uneasily as they carried on this conversation and now addressed Gran. "Your cats are meowing a lot," he said. "Are you sure they don't mind being in the car with us?"

"Oh, they love it," said Gran. "In fact, they can't wait to go on patrol with us. Isn't that right, Scarlett?"

"Absolutely," said Scarlett. "The moment we pull out for our patrol, they practically beg to be let into the car. They're like dogs in that respect, you know, Cliff. Can't wait to join their humans on their trip."

"Gee, and here I always thought cats hated to be in cars," said Cliff as he scratched his scalp. He regarded them a little closer. "The big one doesn't look happy, though. We always had cats, Mindy and I, and I can tell you this one looks decidedly unhappy."

"Oh, you had cats, did you?" asked Gran.

"Yeah, but after the last one passed away, we decided not to get a new one. We're getting on in age, and Mindy didn't think it was a good idea to commit for another fifteen years or so. We may have to move into a nursing home before then, and most of these places don't allow pets, so…"

They all looked up at Cliff with fresh eyes.

"He's a cat person," said Harriet. "I knew it. You can see it in his face. He has a very kind face, doesn't he? The face of a cat person."

"He does have a very kind face," Brutus agreed. "Now I see why he's perfect for the watch. Only cat people are conscientious and selfless enough to join the watch and do good for others without expecting anything in return."

"He is a wonderful man," said Dooley. "The best."

"He's not so bad," said Max, the only one not voicing a full endorsement of the watch's latest recruit.

"Not so bad!" Harriet cried. "Cliff Puckering is probably the greatest person I've ever met. And coming from me, that's saying something. But then I am probably the best judge of character there ever was. Isn't that so, pookie-loo?"

"You are an amazing judge of character," Brutus agreed. "And if you say Cliff Puckering is the greatest human being you ever met, he must be—there's no doubt about it. What do you say, Max?"

But Max wasn't saying much. He muttered something under his breath they couldn't understand, and it added to Dooley's sense that there was something seriously wrong with his best friend. It detracted a lot from the enjoyment he should feel about riding in the car with Gran. So much so that the next couple of hours passed by with him focused on Max so much he hadn't even noticed that Gran had parked her car again and was watching a house across the street intently until his attention was drawn to it by Brutus giving him a slight shove.

"Mh?" he said, waking up from his thought process. "What is it?"

"Gran has seen something suspicious," Brutus said. "Over there."

And when he looked over there, he saw that a couple of men were carrying boxes from some old house and loading them into a white van parked in front of it.

"I don't like it," Gran announced, shaking her head. "Who loads a van in the middle of the night? No law-abiding citizens, that's for sure." And so she unbuckled her belt. "Let's go take a closer look," she said, and before they could stop her, she had stepped out of the car and was making her way over to that van!

CHAPTER 17

We all hopped out of the car in Gran's wake, since we didn't want to see her come to any harm. Even Cliff, our newest recruit, after some hesitation, decided to join the rest of us. Gran and Scarlett were on the front line, hiding behind a bush and watching the men loading the van like hawks, while the four of us decided to move in a little closer since no one ever bothers to worry about the presence of a couple of cats in the vicinity. Which is how I caught a peek into one of the boxes they were carrying into the car. The moment I saw the logo, I couldn't believe my eyes.

"You guys!" I cried excitedly. "It's Franklin Cooper! Franklin Cooper kibble!"

"No way," said Brutus as he also joined me. One of the men had placed a stack of boxes on the sidewalk while his friend loaded them into the van. Which is how we happened to take a closer look at them. And as Brutus pressed his claw against the box under consideration, we both found ourselves staring at the familiar design: it was a bag of Franklin Cooper, all right!

"My god," said Harriet. "I don't believe this. I thought all of the Franklin Cooper was extinct?"

"Apparently not," said Brutus. "Here it is, and looking brand-new as well!"

I wouldn't have said it was brand-new. The bag certainly looked pristine, but as I took a closer look at the date on the bag, I saw that its contents had expired years ago, same as the bags we had found at the house. "They're expired," I told the others.

"Who cares! Expiration dates—"

"Are only suggestions," I said, repeating that tired old dictum. "I know, but that doesn't mean this kibble is still edible."

"Look, if it's good enough for Lucian's queen, it's good enough for us," Brutus argued. "So let's grab a couple of boxes and get out of here!"

But before we could tell Gran to do so, the second man had returned, putting down several more boxes. And when he saw us, he grinned. "Hey, Wayne. Look at these kitties. Looks like they want a piece of that kibble."

"They can't have it," his colleague growled nastily. "Shoo!" he said, kicking at us with his boot. "Get lost, you stupid rats. Get lost, I said!"

And since he didn't look as if he was kidding, we retreated into those same bushes Gran and Scarlett were hiding in and started working on a new plan. For that we wanted to lay our paws on that kibble was a given, even if it was expired!

Of Cliff, there was no sign, which I took as a good thing, since he might have given us away, being a rookie at these delicate operations and all. But then, bold as brass, he suddenly walked up to the two men. "Oh, hey," he said. "What's in those boxes, if you don't mind me asking?"

"None of your business, that's what," Wayne grunted as he

eyed the person with a nasty expression on his face. "Now get lost, old man, before I make you."

"Don't get your panties in a wad," said Cliff with a laugh. "I live around here, you know. So naturally, I'm curious."

"Well, don't be," the second man advised. "It's bad for your health."

Cliff circled back and joined us in the bushes. "Not very friendly, that's for sure," he said.

"They're up to something," said Gran. "I can feel it in my bones."

"There's cat kibble in those boxes," said Scarlett. "Franklin Cooper."

"How do you know?" asked Cliff, much surprised.

For a moment, Scarlett didn't respond. Then she said, "I have perfect vision and I can see from here that there's cat food in those boxes—trust me."

"Cat food, huh? So I guess those bones of yours are mistaken, Vesta."

"No, they're not," Gran assured the man. "Something very rotten is going on here." She then gestured to the four of us, and I could already see which way the wind was blowing.

"Looks like we're going in," I said with a groan. And since there was no saying no to Gran when she had her mind made up, we formed a line and snuck up to the house, glanced around to see if the coast was clear, and then hurried inside. It wasn't long before we discovered where all that kibble was coming from: the man named Wayne came stomping up a rickety set of stairs carrying a couple of heavy boxes and almost tripped over us. We quickly made ourselves scarce by hiding in a side room, and only came out when we were sure that the coast was clear.

"Should we go down there?" asked Harriet the obvious question.

"I'm not sure," I said. "What if we can't get out of there before that guy returns?"

"I say we go and take a look-see," Brutus said.

"And I say that Max should go back and rest in the car," said Dooley. When I gave him a look of exasperation, he said, "Max, you're not well! I can see it, Harriet and Brutus can see it, even Cliff can see it. In fact, you're probably the only one who can't see it! Go lie down in the car, Max!"

"No," I said stubbornly. "I'm perfectly fine!"

"Oh, Max," said Dooley, shaking his head.

And since I wasn't going to have this argument again, I decided to head down those stairs and make it quick, before that brute returned and gave us a closer look at the underside of his boot.

It wasn't long before we realized that the basement in this place was a lot bigger than the one at home. Several rooms forked off the main thoroughfare, and all of them looked as if they had seen better days. Most of them were closed, but one was standing open, and when we carefully padded inside, we discovered that we had hit upon Aladdin's Cave.

From top to bottom, all the way to the ceiling, boxes of Franklin Cooper kibble had been piled up. Hundreds of them—possibly thousands!

"My god!" said Harriet as she looked upon this treasure with awe written all over her features. "You guys! We just hit the jackpot!"

Next to the door, a box stood whose contents had been opened, and since we couldn't restrain ourselves any longer, we all dug in for a nibble. I have to say it tasted as amazingly delicious as I remembered—expiration date or not! And as we went in for seconds, suddenly I thought I heard a noise. And so, quick as a flash, we scrambled out of there, looking for cover. Lucky for us, another door was open, and so we hid in there until the danger had passed.

It took me a while to realize it, but as I stepped back, suddenly my paw touched something lying on the cement floor. And as I glanced down, I found myself staring into the face of a man. Unseeing eyes stared back at me, and if I wasn't mistaken, this man was very dead indeed. The reason wasn't hard to fathom: he had a large dragon sticking out of the side of his head!

CHAPTER 18

I'm not usually a scaredy-cat, or even extremely squeamish, but when I'm confronted with a dead body up close and personal, I can't help but express my surprise and dismay by screaming at the top of my lungs. It's a reflex thing. And so that's what happened. I yelled, and even as I realized my faux-pas, that same unfriendly and cat-hating man came hurrying into the room, flicked on the light, and when he saw himself faced with the same four cats, a sort of grin spread across his face. And as he closed the door behind him, he rolled up his sleeves, clearly eager to teach us a lesson we wouldn't forget.

Now I don't know if you've ever faced four cats locked up in a room with no way out. Well, I have to say we don't like it. In fact, we hate it. And when cats feel cornered, they lash out. It's just something we do. And so by the time the door opened again, this time by the man's compadre, he found the same four cats, the dead man, and his colleague looking like death warmed over and covered in cuts and bruises from top to bottom, his clothes ripped to shreds.

I'm sorry to say we fled the scene, even as both men

screamed up a storm and said some things about us and cats in general that don't bear repeating. Suffice it to say that we were out of that house and back on the street in next to no time, to report to Gran what had happened. I like to think that having snacked on our favorite kibble had given us strength to deal with that bully, but then even without Franklin Cooper we would have acted the same way. Instinct is real!

"A dead man?" asked Gran before she could stop herself. Cliff gave her a strange look. She quickly corrected herself. "He's a dead man!" she said, shaking her fist.

"Who's a dead man?" asked Cliff.

"The guy that threatened my cats," she explained.

"Oh, right," he said, but the look on his face told us that he was puzzled, perhaps even mystified. And when Gran took out her phone and called her son once again, this time to report a crime in progress at that old dilapidated house, and that it may or may not involve a dead body with a dragon sticking out of its head (the last words uttered in an urgent whisper), he frowned even more.

I guess he hadn't heard that old story about Gran being able to talk to her cats.

"Okay, so let's stay here and keep an eye on these men," she suggested, "until the police get here. And make sure they don't get away."

"And how are we going to do that?" asked Cliff.

Now that was a question that would have given a lesser person pause, but to Gran, it only served to unlock the recesses of her mind where she kept her best ideas—or her worst, depending on who you ask. And so when the two men emerged from the house once again, one of them looking as if he'd just been run down by a combine harvester, and continued loading that van, she emerged from behind that bush and walked up to them, even as Cliff hissed, "What are you doing!"

"Oh, heya fellas," said Gran as she joined them. The men exchanged a look of surprise, then eyed her darkly, as they had Cliff. Clearly, they weren't big fans of lookie-loos.

"What do you want?" asked the one we'd had a close encounter with. Someone had gone and dressed his wounds with band-aids, and he was now covered with them.

"You two look like a pair of strong customers," she said. "My car just broke down. Would you mind terribly giving me a push? That shouldn't be any problem for you guys, should it?"

The two men were just about to tell her to take a hike when Scarlett joined them. As usual, she was dressed to impress. She might be her friend's age, but people easily estimate her to be ten years her junior. She had shifted her top a little lower, accentuating her vertiginous cleavage, and had hiked up her skirt, showcasing her long legs.

"Hey fellas," she said in a low and seductive voice. "I see you already met my friend. You two handsome boys wouldn't mind giving us a hand with our car, would you? Breaking down in the middle of nowhere isn't any fun." She gave them her best pout, and the effect was instantaneous.

Drool practically dripped from both men's mouths at the sight of Scarlett, and they dropped everything and hurried after her in the direction of the old red Peugeot Gran likes to drive.

"I don't know what's wrong," said Scarlett. "I held that clutch and shifted it this way and that, and that way and this, but nothing happened." She demonstrated her statement by taking a firm hold of the clutch and vigorously working it. And it was true: nothing at all was happening.

The man named Wayne laughed and said she wasn't doing

it right, and his friend, whose name was Ali, said she was doing it exactly right, and he wouldn't mind if she demonstrated her technique on *his* clutch. There was some general jolliment, and they would have stayed there indefinitely—or at least until the cops arrived—if a woman hadn't emerged from the house and gone in search of them. She was a blond-haired woman in her forties and looked like a forceful type of person. The moment she located the two men, she whistled and yelled, "What do you think you're doing, you idiots! Come back here!"

And I figure the woman must have had some hold over them, for even though she didn't look as attractive as Scarlett did, they instantly jumped to attention and hurried back into the house. It wasn't long before they came out again, carrying more boxes. Accompanying them was the woman, a man I hadn't seen before, and two more men who looked as if they wouldn't mind putting a bullet in a person's head without blinking. They all hopped into that van, and before Gran could think up another one of her schemes, peeled out of there with screeching tires, leaving us sucking in a cloud of dust and diesel fumes.

Ten seconds later, the first police car arrived—too late, of course.

CHAPTER 19

Much to our surprise, the police found not only the dead man we had accidentally discovered but also two more men being held prisoner in that house. One of them was a toy store owner, who possibly had sold the dragon that had killed the other man. And the other guy accused the toy store owner of trying to move the body, along with the woman we had seen making her escape.

It was definitely a complicated puzzle that Chase and his officers were going to have to untangle. It pains me to admit that the only thing that interested us was the fate of that kibble. Those boxes and boxes full of premium kibble. That wonderful, tasty, delicious… Well, you probably catch my drift. As it was, the kibble stood to be confiscated by the police as part of the investigation, though I really didn't see what that poor kibble had done to deserve such a terrible fate. I mean, Franklin Cooper's Premium Pet Food hadn't murdered that poor man, had it? Or locked up the others? So why was it being punished—and why were we being punished, by not being given access to the stuff? It just wasn't fair, we all felt. But then fairness doesn't always go hand in hand with a police investigation.

As it was, Odelia seemed too busy handling things alongside her husband to bother with our repeated pleas to grab at least one of those boxes and take it home with us. And when we approached Gran, who stood eyeing the circus with a critical eye, she said that her hands were tied, even though we could all see that her hands weren't tied at all.

"We have to do something, you guys," said Harriet. "They're going to lock that poor kibble up in the evidence room at the police station if we don't act now."

"What can we do?" asked Brutus. "Chase and Odelia are traipsing all over that house, along with a dozen officers and crime scene people, so there's simply no way for us to gain access and abscond with a couple of boxes. And besides, we're not exactly in the capacity to carry those boxes out of there."

"Gran could do it," said Harriet.

"Yes, but we asked, and she said no," I reminded her.

We cut a glance over at the old woman, who seemed to feel that she wasn't being given enough credit for her big discovery that this seemingly innocuous house contained such a dark secret. No one had thanked her yet, and that didn't sit well with her.

"They're going to take all the credit," she told her friend Scarlett. "Just you wait and see. It's going to be all over the paper tomorrow: your intrepid reporter has discovered a dead body and two prisoners being held in some old house somewhere. With not a single mention of the neighborhood watch."

"Odelia wouldn't do that," said Scarlett. "Would she?"

"Oh, she will. That's how it's going down. When all the while it was us who hit upon this place. And if it hadn't been for the cats, we wouldn't even have known about that dead body." She looked over at us and gave us a nod of appreciation. "Credit should be given where credit is due," she emphasized.

"I wonder if that dead body and these brown little pellets got anything to do with those punks on my street," said Cliff, who was following his own train of thought. "I mean, look at them. They're almost identical." He was holding in his hand one of the pieces of kibble that we had found in the basement. And as he held it up, I could see why he would say that. It did indeed look very similar to the little brown pills those punks were selling on his street.

"Impossible," said Gran. "I mean, those kids were selling drugs, no doubt about it. But these aren't drugs, Cliff. This is cat kibble. And as we all know, cat kibble isn't drugs."

"I know, but it looks very similar," he insisted. But since he had to admit that there was no way that anyone could possibly mistake cat kibble for narcotics, he decided to let it drop. "I have to say this night has been a real eye-opener. And I want to thank the two of you for allowing me to tag along."

"You're very welcome," said Gran. "Though if you think that every night is like this, you're very much mistaken. Mostly it's just the two of us driving around and looking at quiet empty streets where nothing happens. Isn't that right, Scarlett?"

Scarlett nodded. "It's very rare that something actually does happen," she agreed. "So I guess you were in luck tonight, Cliff," she added as she clapped the old man on the back.

"I guess so," he said, looking relieved that his decision to join the neighborhood watch hadn't ended in him being attacked, shot, knifed, or otherwise hurt. "My wife told me I shouldn't do it, you know," he confessed. "She said it was too dangerous. And I can see now that she was right. It is dangerous. But if we hadn't done what we did, those poor suckers would still be locked up down there—or worse, they might have been killed by now."

"Yeah, I have no doubt whatsoever that they meant to have them killed," Gran agreed. "Just like that other man that we found. Which means that they could have killed us."

The three of them gulped a little as the realization hit them that their lives had been in danger when they confronted those men loading that van. Wayne and Ali were probably stone-cold killers!

We listened for a while longer, then focused on the matter at hand: how to get our paws on that kibble! "Okay, I can only see one other way," said Harriet now. "We will have to recruit the only person capable of pulling this off—and we'll have to make it worth her while."

"And who is this person?" asked Brutus.

"Marge, of course. We've asked Gran and she flat-out refused. We asked Odelia, but she's too busy, and besides, she doesn't want to make police evidence disappear."

"And she has this weird hang-up about expiration dates," Dooley reminded us.

"So the only other person we can talk to about this is Marge. And if she's not willing to do us this little favor, I'm afraid we're sunk, you guys. And we may never have another taste of Franklin Cooper!"

We all thought about that for a moment. The problem is that Marge, even more than her mother and her daughter, is the epitome of the law-abiding citizen. So it was extremely unlikely that she would be willing to assist us in laying our greedy little paws on a couple of boxes of that kibble.

"What can we give Marge that would make her play ball?" asked Brutus. "There must be something, so think, you guys. Think!"

For some reason, he was looking at me as he spoke these

words, but try as I might, I couldn't think of anything that might induce Marge to play along with our designs.

"I think I've got it," suddenly Dooley piped up, and the look on his face told us that he might have hit on a pretty sweet idea.

"What is it?" asked Harriet eagerly. By now she was crediting Franklin Cooper kibble as being conducive to her fine fur and the remarkable glow it possessed and wanted more of the stuff—much, much more.

"It's simple," he said. "We tell her that if she doesn't get us that kibble, we'll run away from home!"

We all stared at him, then shook our heads collectively. "Been there, done that," said Harriet, summing things up nicely. She was right. We had already tried that, and even though it had worked—more or less—it hadn't been a fun experience for us. Running away from home is all fine and dandy, but where can you go without losing those creature comforts we had all become accustomed to?

"There must be something else," said Harriet musingly. "Something that will make Marge decide to play ball."

And as we pondered possible solutions to our problem, I saw that one of the police officers had started carrying the boxes of kibble from the house and loading them into a police van. "Oh, you guys!" I said and pointed to the van. "It's happening! They're taking it away!"

We looked at the procession of officers now forming a kind of conga line and transferring those dozens and dozens of boxes of fine kibble—possibly hundreds or maybe even a metric ton of the stuff—from the house and gradually filling up that van, to be taken to the police station evidence room, most likely never to be seen or heard from again, and I felt a distinct sense of sorrow washing over me.

"Too bad we can't drive," said Harriet. "Or we could simply jump behind the wheel and drive that van to

Harrington Street and transfer those boxes to Tex's garden house."

"To dip into that stash any time we please," said Brutus dreamily.

"A stash like that would last us a lifetime," said Dooley. "Several lifetimes. Eternity!"

And as we all looked on, salivating at this appealing scenario, suddenly I got an idea. I don't know if it was my brain still suffering from that heatwave, but at that moment, it seemed like the best idea ever!

But when I explained my idea to the others, they all seemed to think it was as great as I thought it was. And so it was decided. The four musketeers would ride again—literally!

CHAPTER 20

It had been quite the eventful night for Cliff Puckering. In fact, he couldn't remember ever having lived through so much excitement in his life, and he already knew that Mindy would think he was exaggerating when he told her. But as he stood watching the frenzied police activity surrounding the house on Alhola Street, what happened next was so outrageous that he had to blink a few times, and even then he could barely believe it was actually happening.

The police van, having been filled with boxes dragged from the house, had been loaded to capacity, and when the final couple of boxes had been stuffed into the vehicle, the police officers tasked with the loading closed the door and got ready to drive off. But before the driver took up his position behind the wheel, he decided to enjoy a quick smoke. And as he did, leaning against the van, Cliff saw the four cats belonging to Vesta sneak into the van. Two of them took up position on the floor, one of them behind the wheel, and one jumped on top of the dashboard. And as he stared at the strange scene, suddenly the van started to move! And as the officer leaning against it became aware of this, he shouted, "Hey! Stop that!"

But even he was so surprised to see that four cats were driving his van that he just stood there, rooted to the spot, his mouth hanging open and his cigarette falling from his fingers.

"What the…" he muttered.

And before he had a chance to get a grip on himself, the van was already gaining speed, and going at a pretty fast clip, heading in the direction of the end of the street. And as Cliff watched it turn the corner, the officer finally shook himself out of his stupor and started running after it. "Come back here!" he yelled. "Come back here, you… cats!"

Vesta and Scarlett, who hadn't noticed a thing, now joined Cliff again, and when they saw the cop run the hundred-yard dash along the street, Vesta asked, "What got into him?"

"It's your cats," said Cliff, finally regaining his power of speech.

"What about my cats?" asked Vesta with a frown.

"They took…" He gulped a few times. "They took…"

"Yes?" she asked impatiently. "Just spit it out, man!"

"They took the van and drove off with it!"

For a moment, Vesta just looked at him as if he'd lost his mind, which he now figured was definitely a possibility. Then she laughed heartily. "Yeah, right. Stop pulling my leg, Puckering!"

"Yes, you don't have to crack jokes, Cliff," said Scarlett, "just to get in our good graces."

"You did a great job tonight," said Vesta, offering a rare compliment. "In fact, I think you're exactly the kind of person we've been looking for. So consider yourself accepted into the watch, buddy boy!"

He should have been happy, but the van with the cats

behind the wheel still preyed on his mind. So instead of thanking the woman for her vote of approval, he repeated, "But your cats! They just drove off with that van!"

Now Vesta's frown deepened, and she growled, "Enough about my cats already, Cliff."

"Yeah, it's not funny anymore, Cliff," Scarlett added. "Vesta loves those cats, you know."

"I know!" he said. "And now they're zooming along at thirty miles an hour through the streets of Hampton Cove, heading God knows where, with a policeman on their tail!"

For a moment, the two women didn't say anything, then finally Vesta seemed to understand that he wasn't kidding but that it was all too real. "My cats are driving a van?" she asked in feeble tones.

"Yes, they are! The fat one was on the floor, pressing down on the accelerator, that small fluffy one next to him busying himself with the brake, the black one is behind the wheel, and the Persian is sitting on the dash, presumably to tell the others where to go!"

"Oh, my God!" said Vesta, clutching her little white curls. "Quick, we have to go after them!"

And so they found themselves back in that little old Peugeot and in hot pursuit of a van filled with what could only be termed as stolen loot, driven by four very determined cats!

"I should have known they were up to something!" said Vesta as she sat hunched over the wheel while her car was whining in complaint at the harsh treatment she was subjecting it to. "They kept going on and on about that kibble, so I should have stopped that nonsense dead in its tracks!"

Cliff wondered how the woman could have known that her cats were complaining about the kibble, but then he guessed that after having lived with those cats for years, she had developed a sixth sense about what it was that they wanted.

"Don't blame yourself," said Scarlett. "You couldn't possibly have known they were planning on stealing a police van."

"Oh, God!" said Vesta. "They'll arrest them, won't they? And put them in the pound!"

"No, they won't," said Scarlett.

"They'll arrest them and throw away the key!"

"No, they won't," said her friend, but she didn't sound very sure of herself.

"They won't get far," said Cliff. "Cats aren't capable of driving a car. Are they?"

These were some very special cats, though. That much he'd been able to ascertain, even in the short time he'd known them. So maybe they were some kind of supercats?

"I just hope they don't drive into something," said Vesta. "A house or something."

"Or another vehicle," Scarlett murmured. She was clutching her seat as Vesta drove like a bat out of hell and didn't look very at ease that they wouldn't hit another vehicle themselves.

Before long, they had overtaken the police officer, who stood panting by the side of the road and looked a little overheated after all of his exertions.

When the cop saw the mother of his superior officer pass him by, he held up his hand to hitch a ride, but Vesta simply ignored him and kept on going.

"Aren't you going to let him ride along?" asked Scarlett.

"And give him a chance to arrest my cats? No way!" said the old lady.

It wasn't long before they got a bead on the missing van. It was dangerously lurching across the road, and it reminded Cliff of that time he'd seen a drunk driver almost mowing down a group of pedestrians. Good thing it was the middle of the night, and no pedestrians were anywhere in sight.

"There!" said Vesta. "We got them!"

She took the car to the limits of what it could do, and judging from the smoke wafting from the hood, they wouldn't be able to keep this up much longer.

"Easy now, Vesta," said Scarlett. "You don't want to bump into them."

But Vesta wasn't listening. She had got a kind of mulish look on her face that Cliff was starting to recognize as not a good sign.

"Vesta?" said Scarlett. "Slow down. You're going to hit them in the rear."

But the car wasn't slowing down. If anything, it was speeding up!

"Vesta!" Scarlett yelled. "Watch out!"

They were bumper to bumper with the van in front of them, and as the van lurched to the right, Vesta's car lurched to the left, and she quickly overtook the cats. And as they were driving side by side, Cliff saw that the formation was still intact: that chubby red one was sitting on the accelerator, his friend on the brake, while the black cat was steering the vehicle, and the white one was giving directions on how to drive. They all looked a little terrified, he thought, but then that was probably to be expected, as this might be a first for them.

It definitely was a first for him!

Scarlett had rolled down the window, and Vesta yelled, "Stop that car at once!"

He didn't know what the cats yelled back. There seemed to be a lot of meowing going on, and as Vesta repeated her demand, suddenly the van pulled ahead and left them in the dust.

The big red cat had pushed the pedal all the way down to

the metal by allowing gravity to do its job, and the cats were hauling ass. The little red Peugeot's engine was now barking up dark fumes, and with a final cough, a minor explosion, and a death rattle, it gave up the ghost.

The chase was over, and it looked like the cats had won.

CHAPTER 21

Look, it was a spur-of-the-moment kind of thing, all right? And in my defense, my brain wasn't firing on all cylinders, and I blame that darn heatwave. All in all, though, it seemed like the best chance we had of securing that kibble for ourselves. What good would it do for that wonderful stuff to be languishing in a police lock-up? Nothing whatsoever! And so when we saw the chance, we took it. If it made us fugitives from justice, so be it. Though truth be told, I didn't think about the consequences when I proposed the idea. The only thing I thought of was that I would be able to taste that fine, fine kibble once again.

And since we didn't have a lot of time before that police officer finished his cigarette, we decided to take action and take it right now. I jumped on the gas, Dooley on the brakes, Harriet said she would act as our lookout, and Brutus had the most important task of all: to tame that steering wheel! It wasn't easy, but somehow we managed. The hard part was negotiating those corners. Every time we had to take a corner, I had to ease up on the gas, Dooley had to touch down on the brake—but not too much or we'd stall—and

Harriet had to direct her mate to make sure he didn't hit any parked cars or other obstacles.

"To the right!" she yelled. "More! More! MORE!"

"I'm trying, I'm trying!" Brutus yelled back. "But this steering wheel is real sticky!"

"We should have washed it," Dooley suggested.

"I don't mean sticky, sticky!" said Brutus. "I mean it doesn't do what I want it to do."

"It's these old vans," Harriet knew. "They don't use power steering, you know."

"I'll say," said Brutus, huffing and puffing as he tried to get the van to go in the right direction. "Are we there yet?"

"Where are we going, actually?" asked Harriet. "I forgot to ask, Max."

"Let's not go home," I suggested. "Odelia won't be happy. In fact, none of our humans will be happy. Let's drive this van straight to Blake's Field and leave it there for now, hidden in the bushes. Then when the time comes that we have recruited a human to do the heavy lifting, we'll ask them to transfer the kibble to a safe location, where only we can get at it."

"Great idea," said Brutus. "Though what human is going to help us, I don't know."

"Like I said, the only person I can think of is Marge. But we have to find some leverage. Something we can use on her. Something she desperately wants and only we are in a position to give."

It was a tough one, and I hadn't figured it out yet, but if we were going to stand a chance at having access to our kibble from now on and for the rest of our lives, we needed to find a way to induce Marge to give us a helping hand. Odelia was a spent force, and so was Gran, so the only person left was Marge.

PURRFECT KIBBLE

"There's one other person who understands us," said Dooley.

"There is?" I asked as I brought my weight to bear on the gas.

"Of course. Grace," he said. "And I'm sure she'll want to help."

"Grace isn't big and strong enough to carry these boxes," I told my friend.

"No, but she has friends. Lots of friends. All of those boys and girls at the daycare."

It certainly was an idea we should entertain, I thought. But since I had my paws full trying to keep the car going at a steady rate of speed, I put it on the back burner for now.

"Look who's there," said Harriet suddenly. And when I glanced over, I saw through the open driver's door—we hadn't been able to close it for obvious reasons—that Gran was driving right next to us and shouting something.

"What is she saying, Max?" asked Dooley.

"I think she wants us to stop," I said.

"Are we going to stop?" asked Harriet.

"Of course not," said Brutus. "She'll just want us to surrender our kibble, and that is something we'll never do, you guys."

"Absolutely," I agreed.

"This kibble is ours!" Harriet said.

"Maybe you can push down on the gas," Dooley suggested.

And so I put my full weight, which is considerable, I have to admit, on that pedal, making it go all the way down to the floor. The van sprang forward, and soon we had left Gran and Scarlett and Cliff in the dust.

"Onward and upward!" Brutus yelled.

"I feel the wind in my hair, papa bear!" said Harriet. "And it's glorious!"

"I know exactly how you feel, lemon drop!" said Brutus. "It's the need for speed!"

The need to make sure no one got their hands on our kibble, to be more precise.

Before long, we had arrived at Blake's Field, and Harriet told me to ease up on the throttle and so after we had jumped the curb, we traversed the derelict piece of land, rife with weeds and bushes and brambles, and the van bumped and bounced its way to the center of that jungle-like area, until we had reached the most overgrown part of it. Finally, we rolled to a halt, and when we got out, I saw that the van was perfectly secluded and would never be found by anyone, unless you knew what to look for.

"Excellent," said Harriet. She held up her paw. "Amazing job, you guys!"

And so we all shared a high-five on a job well done.

"And now for the hard part," said Brutus.

I nodded. "Denial is our friend," I reminded them.

"Deny, deny, deny," Harriet agreed.

"I know nothing!" said Dooley.

And so we commenced our short trek home, where our humans awaited, possibly not all that happy with us. I just hoped Gran wouldn't have told the others about what she had seen. She was the only one who could give us trouble—apart from that one police officer, of course.

CHAPTER 22

Freddie had really been through the wringer. And it all began when he accidentally bumped into that woman's car. What a bit of bad luck that was! After the police freed him from his momentary prison cell and he told them everything he knew about his captors and their motivations for locking him up, they finally took him home, where his parents were awaiting him.

He had phoned them from the police station and filled them in on what was going on, managing to allay their concerns about his well-being with a few words. When he walked through the door, it was clear that he hadn't done a very good job, for his mom had been crying, and his dad looked extremely worried too.

"I'm fine, I'm fine!" he said when Mom hugged him so close that for a moment he couldn't breathe.

"Never do that to us again!" she said.

He smiled. "I'll try not to." Though he couldn't promise never to run into that woman again, he would definitely give it his best shot. The very kind police officer who had interviewed him had asked him to look at mug shots, but unfortunately he hadn't been able to pick her out of their sizable parade of jailbirds—old and new. The description he gave them hadn't helped, as it had been too vague, he realized. How many attractive blond-haired forty-year-old women were there? Probably a lot!

He just hoped that they would find her, and make sure she didn't come after him—again.

For a few moments, he sat at the kitchen table with his mom and dad, with Mom feeding him some of her mashed potatoes with hash browns—homemade, of course—and a cup of hot pumpkin soup. He had to tell his tale a couple of times over, and even then they found it very hard to believe that he would have had a brush with death like that. By the time he was ready for bed, he was so tired that the moment his head hit the pillow he was out like a light.

Which is probably why he didn't notice the person looking in through his bedroom window and giving him the evil eye. If he had been awake, he would have recognized her as the same woman he'd been dancing the tango with all day, and she did not look very happy.

* * *

FOR YEARS, Rebekka had been able to lead a life free from any entanglements with the law. Even though her dad had had his run-ins with the constabulary, no member of the family had ever done time, which was quite amazing when you thought about it since they had been operating on the wrong side of the law for all those same years. And now that Dad was old and ready for the nursing home and Mom was the same way, and the younger generation had taken over, she knew they were facing a great risk.

Like in any business, the transition from one generation to the next always represents a danger. Their dad had often warned them about it and had told them to be extra careful when the time came that he announced his retirement and handed the reins of the family business to his two sons and one daughter. But even he, a clever operator, hadn't expected that it would actually be Rebekka who would jeopardize them all, since she had always been the clever one. The careful one. The one who was destined to take over from her dad.

And now this mess, which was entirely of her own making. If she hadn't decided to help the toy store guy hide that body, this would never have happened. And if she hadn't tussled with that annoying little twerp Freddie Tottman, he wouldn't even know what she looked like. Lucky for her she always wore her wig when she was out and about attending to her family's business interests.

And if they thought she was going down without a fight they had another thing coming. The family might have lost a large part of their stash, but she knew exactly where she could get more. Plenty more. An endless supply, in fact. And even though they might have to lay low for a while, this wasn't the end.

She glanced in at that annoying man who she held responsible for much of the trouble the family now found itself in and had to resist the urge to climb in through his window and murder him in his bed right then and there. She knew it would provide a sense of satisfaction, but ultimately would only serve to get her into more trouble than it was worth.

At least she knew where he lived now.

She got back into the car, and as Dirk raced away with squealing tires, he asked, "Is it him?"

She nodded. "Yup, it's him all right. Freddie Tottman. Still lives with his folks, apparently."

"We can't touch him—you know that, right?"

"Oh, I know that," she said as she glanced out of the window. "I'm not stupid, Dirk."

"So what are you going to do?" asked her husband.

"I'm going to let some time pass. And once he thinks he's safe, I'm going to strike. I'm going to make him pay for what he did to us, that annoying nitwit."

"I didn't mean the kid. I meant the business," he said with a touch of irritation.

"Oh, that. Well, let's just say I've got a plan." And as she told him some of the details, she could see the sense of irritation drain from his system, to be replaced by a look of sheer admiration.

CHAPTER 23

To say that we got a warm reception would be an understatement. But much to our astonishment, that warm reception only involved a single person in the Poole household: Gran.

"What do you think you're doing!" she hissed the moment we passed through the pet flap and into the Poole kitchen. "You could have gotten yourselves killed!"

We glanced around, and when we discovered that the welcome committee only consisted of Gran, we breathed a sigh of relief.

"Didn't you... tell the others?" asked Harriet.

Gran frowned. "Now why would I go and tell the others that our cats stole a police car and drove off with it? Do you think I'm crazy? They'd probably put you in the pound."

"So Odelia doesn't know?" I asked.

"Or Marge?" asked Dooley.

Gran shook her head. "*I* know," she said, giving us a stern-faced look. "And I hope you will never pull such a crazy stunt again. Is that understood!"

We all nodded shamefacedly as she poured her anger out

on us. But when we looked up again, we saw that she had tears in her eyes.

"My cats, driving a car. If I wasn't so angry I would hug you," she said. Harriet frowned and exchanged a look of confusion with me. And as Dooley jumped up on his human's lap, and butted his head against her chin, she sniffed, "I'm so proud of you guys. Stealing a police car and taking off with it. I don't think I've ever been so proud of anyone in my life."

It was definitely a mixed message she was giving us here. So was she either angry or proud. It was hard to tell which, so finally we settled on somewhere in the middle. Looked like she was on a sliding scale between angry and ecstatic. Proud and upset. Only humans could pull off something like that.

"So what did you do with the van?" she asked.

"We parked it in Blake's Field," I said.

"It wasn't easy," said Brutus as he flexed his paws. "In fact, I'm still feeling the strain. You should definitely tell your son that he should renovate his car park. Did you know that his police vehicles don't have power steering?"

Gran's expression shifted again. "You really scared me, you know," she said. "You could have ended up crashing into a tree, or a car, or ended up driving off a cliff."

"There are no cliffs in downtown Hampton Cove," I reminded her.

"You know what I mean," she said as she sniffled some more.

"What did Cliff say?" asked Brutus.

The realization that there had been witnesses to our crime had come as quite a shock to us, and if they weren't going to be as lenient as Gran, we might still get in trouble, so we awaited her response with bated breath.

"Oh, he's fine with it," Gran assured us. "I told him to keep his mouth shut if he ever wanted to stand a chance at being part of the watch and he said he wouldn't tell a living soul."

"And what about that policeman?" asked Brutus.

Gran smiled. "It's all about thinking ahead and being proactive, you guys. So I simply told Chase that I'd seen that guy smoking some highly suspicious substance, and that he shouldn't believe a word he said. I think that should suffice to nip that particular story in the bud."

"We still need someone to unload that van for us," Harriet tried, but Gran wasn't having it.

"Are you seriously asking me to unload a bunch of stolen loot from a stolen police vehicle?"

"Well… yes," said Harriet.

But Gran shook her head. "That's where I draw the line. I don't want you to get into trouble, so I won't tell anyone about what you've been up to. But I'm not going to unload that van for you, is that understood?"

We sighed unhappily. Looked like we'd have to find another volunteer. And since it was way past Gran's bedtime, she said she'd turn in for the night, but not before admonishing us not to steal any more police vans that night.

"We won't," Harriet promised.

Gran smiled and patted her on the cheek. "So proud of you," she murmured, going through another quick reversal, and then passed out of the kitchen and upstairs for a good night's sleep after all the excitement she had lived through that day.

For a moment we pondered what to do. And since I already knew that the following day would mainly consist of me passed out on the basement floor trying to keep my body heat in check, I suggested that we go to cat choir while we had the chance and while the night was still young and the air fresh and cool.

And so it was decided. And I have to say that when we

arrived, loud cheers rang out all around us. Maybe human witnesses had been rare on our passage through town with that stolen police vehicle, but as usual there had been plenty of pet witnesses, and as it turned out, we were the talk of the town.

"The fast and the furious!" said Kingman as he clapped his hands in a tribute to our daring stunt. "Though I'm not sure who the fast and who the furious is."

"I'm the fast, of course," said Harriet. "And Brutus is the furious."

"Credit where credit is due," said Brutus modestly. "Max was the one pushing down on the accelerator, so he's probably the fastest cat this town has ever known."

"If you hadn't steered the car in the right direction and kept it under control the entire time," I said, "we would probably be lying in a ditch somewhere, or parked in a store window."

"And if Dooley hadn't applied his judgment to that brake, we would never have been able to take those corners," said Harriet. She smiled. "Cooperation is key here, you guys. I couldn't have done it without you. We all worked as a team."

"So it takes four cats to replace one human driver, does it?" asked Shanille.

"I guess so," I said. And since I was feeling magnanimous, I decided to invite all of our friends to share a nice dinner at our place—once we had managed to move those bags of kibble to a safe place. I could see that Harriet didn't agree with me, but I knew there was enough kibble in those bags to feed all of cat choir many times over, so the offer stood and was accepted with loud cheers all around.

CHAPTER 24

We attended a meeting the next day in Odelia's uncle's office where the events of the night before were being scrutinized, as well as some of the conclusions that Chase and Odelia had reached. And even though I had been reluctant to comply when Odelia invited the four of us to attend the meeting, her promise that we could ride in Chase's car, which has an AC unit installed, and that the Mayor had splurged on AC units for the police station, so we wouldn't expire from the heat, made me change my mind and decide to accept her invitation.

"I think it's safe to say that we've hit upon what might very well be the weirdest bust in the history of this town," said the Chief as he studied a small sampling of kibble on his desk. He picked up a single pellet and studied it for a moment, then held it under his nose. "Are you sure about this, Chase?"

"Absolutely, boss," said the detective. "Lab tests have confirmed that this is the stuff being dealt all over town, though mainly in the area around Gillard Street, as we have already ascertained."

"As my mother has ascertained, you mean," said Uncle Alec with a grunt.

The four of us shared a look of confusion. "That is Franklin Cooper kibble, isn't it?" asked Brutus.

"That's right," said Odelia. "It's the kibble we found in the basement of the house on Alhola Street last night. And it's also the same kibble that was taken off the drug dealers arrested last night on Gillard Street, after Gran reported dealers being active in that part of the town."

"Homeowners had been complaining about it also," Chase reminded us. "But until now, nothing linked those dealers with... this stuff."

"But... kibble isn't drugs, surely?" I asked with a laugh.

Odelia gave me a look of concern. "Lab tests have also confirmed that the Franklin Cooper kibble contains a substance that is highly addictive. Possibly the reason that kibble was so popular when it first came out and remained popular all throughout its history."

"It's definitely cause for concern," Chase chimed in. "The kibble being examined contains a substance called Plakka, which as we all know is an extremely dangerous designer drug, which may go a long way to explain why people who consume this particular kibble experience a feeling of high and exhilaration that lasts for a short time before they find themselves in need of another fix."

"So... this kibble has been spiked with a narcotic?" asked Uncle Alec.

Chase nodded. "It also contains what it says on the label, of course. Poultry, beef, brown rice, vitamins and minerals. But yes, for some reason, the Franklin Cooper people found it necessary to spike their kibble with Plakka."

"Was this the reason that the factory was closed down by the FDA, you think?" asked Uncle Alec.

"Almost certainly yes," said the detective. "Though as we all know, the real reason was never disclosed, but I have it on good authority that this was indeed the main reason for the shutdown."

"So the factory was closed for a reason," said the Chief, nodding. "But how did this kibble end up on the street is what I would like to know."

"Back when the Franklin Cooper factory was shut down, the FDA ordered all of the remaining kibble to be destroyed," Odelia explained. "But some of the workers must have realized they could do a good deal, and so instead of destroying the kibble, they offloaded the stuff in bulk on some buyers."

"And apparently a large batch ended up in the hands of a gang of drug dealers."

"It was a great deal for them," said Odelia. "Since the street value of a seven-pound bag of Franklin Cooper is around forty thousand now, with a single pellet selling for about a buck. They bought up all of the remaining stock at a bargain and are getting extremely rich now by pushing it on their users."

"So these people are actually popping pet kibble now?" asked Odelia's uncle, greatly surprised.

"Taking it in pill form or grinding it up and sniffing or smoking it," Chase confirmed. "It's not as strong as pure Plakka, of course, but even in diluted form the lab says it's some pretty potent stuff."

"What happened to the stock that was confiscated from that house last night?" asked Uncle Alec.

As we shared another look, Odelia said, "We're not sure. The officer in charge of that van claims that the cats took off with it."

"Clearly he'd been smoking some of that kibble himself," Chase scoffed. "High as a kite."

"We think that gang members must have returned and stolen that van," said Odelia as she gave me a reassuring pat on the head. "It represented a ridiculous sum of money."

"Brazen," said Uncle Alec, nodding. "Extremely brazen."

"Witnesses have told us that Gran tried to catch them," said Odelia. "But when I asked her about it, she said that unfortunately they got away."

"Ma should be more careful," said Uncle Alec, shaking his head. "Chasing after a couple of hardened gangsters is not the work of the neighborhood watch."

"Max, are we hardened gangsters now?" asked Dooley quietly.

"Looks like it," I whispered back.

He gulped. "And drug addicts, too, by the sound of things!"

I had to swallow once or twice at that kernel of information as well. Did that mean that the four of us were addicts now? It was true that ever since we had eaten from that kibble we couldn't stop thinking about it. I thought it was because it was so delicious, but now it seemed as if something more pernicious was going on. Effectively, we had become hooked on the stuff!

"So you see?" said Odelia as she gave us a stern-faced look. "There's a reason I didn't want you to have that kibble and why I decided to throw it in the trash. It's not good for you."

"You threw it on your dad's compost heap," Chase reminded her.

Odelia slung a distraught hand to her face. "I have to tell him. He'll have to get rid of it again."

"No need," I said somberly. "The ants have stolen it."

"The ants?" asked Odelia. "But you should tell them it's bad for them."

"Oh, trust me, I will," I promised. Though I didn't think Lucian would be impressed.

"Okay, so where are we on arresting this gang of kibble dealers?" asked Uncle Alec as he placed his hands flat on his desk. "Any progress?"

"Nothing," said Chase as he shook his head. "They seem to have vanished into thin air."

"What about the gang leader? This blond-haired woman everyone claims is in charge?"

"No ID yet, I'm afraid," said Chase. "Felix Bennett claims her name is Rita Watts, but I have reason to believe she gave him a false name, for whatever reason. She's not in our database, that's for sure."

"Chase had the kid that was found locked up in the basement look at mug shots," Odelia explained. "But nothing. Looks like she's never been arrested and has never been on the police radar before."

"He did say she looked vaguely familiar," Chase reminded her. "Though he couldn't place her."

"Neither could Gran," said Odelia, "or Scarlett or that new watch member, um…"

"Cliff Puckering," Chase supplied helpfully.

Uncle Alec shook his head. "Drugged kibble. What is the world coming to?"

Chase grinned. "You know, we could call it dribble. Short for drugged kibble. Get it? Dribble? Drugged…" When both his wife and his boss eyed him stoically, he muttered, "Yeah, I guess it's not that funny."

"What is drivel, Max?" asked Dooley.

But Uncle Alec seemed to have had enough of the meeting and he tapped his desk smartly. "Okay, people," he said. "I won't keep you. Get a bead on this gang and do it fast. We want this poison off our streets and that gang behind bars where it belongs."

And so the meeting was adjourned, and the four of us left to do a little soul-searching. Did we still want to pursue our plan to safeguard the kibble we had secured last night? Or did we want to destroy it and get rid of it once and for all? Talk about a tough decision!

CHAPTER 25

Franklin Cooper was happy to receive another message from Patsy, but when he opened the message, he saw that it wasn't his granddaughter who had written it but her mother. In it, Melanie said that she had no wish to get into an argument with him, but that the stipulations of the court order were very clear: no contact. And that she hoped he would respect those stipulations.

He sagged in his armchair, and as his phone fell from his hand, he wondered if he would ever see his grandchildren again. He had a feeling he wouldn't. Not if their mom and dad had anything to do with it.

As he pondered these unpleasant thoughts, the door to his room swung open, and one of the orderlies walked in. It was Steven, who was one of the nicer ones.

"Hey, Steven," he said somberly.

Steven pushed a trolley into the room, carrying his breakfast, and when he saw the old man's face, gave him a look of concern. "Franklin, what's wrong, my man?"

"Oh, nothing," he said, wondering if he should share his

innermost thoughts with this man, who was essentially a stranger.

"Is it your granddaughter?" asked Steven, and Franklin remembered how he had been so excited after Patsy had written him that message that he hadn't been able to control himself and had told the orderly all about it.

"Yeah, her mom has found out, and she's just sent me a strongly worded message that I'm not to have any contact with Patsy or Tamara. Court's orders," he grimaced. "Looks like I won't be paying a visit to their school for Grandparents' Day after all."

"Oh, but that's such a shame!" said the burly orderly, coming over and putting an arm around his stooped shoulder. "Do you want me to have a talk with her? I mean, maybe I can change her mind?"

"I doubt it," he said. "It's my son, you see. He doesn't want me anywhere near his family." And maybe Franklin Jr. was right. After what had happened at the factory, he probably had a point in not wanting his dad to spend time with his two girls. Though it still struck him as harsh.

"I've got some news that will cheer you up," said Steven. "You've got a new neighbor! And he's a very nice man. His name is Quinton Banyard, and he used to work in construction. And I have a feeling you two will get along great, since you used to run your own company as well, didn't you, Franklin?"

"Yeah, I did," he said, straightening a little. In spite of its inglorious ending, he still retained a sense of pride in his achievements. "The biggest pet food company in the country. Bigger than Purina or Hills."

"I remember my mom used to buy Franklin Cooper pet food," said Steven. "She always said it was the best, and her cats loved it. Couldn't get enough of the stuff."

He nodded. Good thing the FDA had never disclosed

what exactly was wrong with the food, or his reputation would have taken an even bigger hit than it had. Part of the deal he had made in exchange for giving them the full picture of how the factory had operated.

"Look, why don't you go and say hi to Quinton?" Steven suggested. "Trust me—you'll feel much better if you have a friend in this place. We all need friends, Franklin. Especially you."

He knew that Steven meant 'Especially when you've been abandoned by your family,' and he appreciated the gesture, but he wasn't in the mood to meet anyone just then, and he told Steven as much.

"Well, maybe later then," said the orderly, who was always upbeat, something Franklin admired about the guy. "Eat your breakfast, and I'll be back in a jiffy. How does that sound?"

"Glorious," he said with a weak smile and started on the 'breakfast of champions,' as Steven always called it. He wasn't hungry, but he still forced himself to finish the whole plate: toast and scrambled eggs and a sausage with some hash browns on the side. It was indeed a breakfast of champions, even though he was a fallen champion now. Even his colleagues in the pet food industry regarded him like something stuck to the bottom of their shoe and hadn't invited him to any of their meetings, which at one point he used to chair. Only one of the many official positions he had proudly championed back in the day.

And as he finished his coffee, the door opened again, and an old man walked in. He looked around a little uncertainly, then directed a strange look at Franklin. "This is my room?" he asked. "Isn't it?"

"No, this is my room," he said. "You must be Quinton?"

"That's right," said the old man, who was using a cane to get around. "Are you sure this isn't my room?"

"Your room is right next door," he said helpfully and got

up with some effort. "I'll show you." He held out his hand. "My name is Franklin, and I'm your new neighbor."

A pair of watery eyes fastened themselves on him. "Oh, is that right?"

"Here, let me show you to your room," he said.

"Thanks…" He gave him a sheepish look. "I forgot your name."

"Franklin," he said, and had a feeling he would probably be repeating this a few more times before it stuck.

He took the man next door, and as he opened the door, saw that a dark-haired woman of attractive aspect and a man with curly hair sat waiting for them. "Dad?" said the woman, immediately getting up. "Where have you been?"

"He walked into my room," said Franklin. "A simple mistake."

The woman gave him a grateful smile. "Dad hasn't been feeling well lately," she explained. "He gets confused sometimes."

"That's all right," said Franklin graciously. "Happens to all of us."

"Thanks, Mr…"

"Cooper," said Franklin, holding out his hand. "Franklin Cooper."

He thought he detected a trace of recognition on the woman's face and was proud that his name still rang a bell, though he always had to wonder if it was because, once upon a time, he'd produced the most popular pet kibble in the country or because of the scandal.

"Franklin Cooper, as in the pet food brand?" she asked.

He nodded. "One and the same."

"Oh, but I loved your stuff. We have dogs," she explained. "And they adored your kibble."

"We couldn't drag enough bags into the house," her

husband said with a warm smile. "Too bad you stopped making it."

"Yeah, what happened?" asked the woman.

The dreaded question, but by now he had his answer ready.

"I retired from the business," he said. "And since my son didn't want to follow in my footsteps, I tried to sell the business, but unfortunately found no takers." He shrugged. "What are you going to do?"

"Too bad," said the woman. "Dad was in business. He would have bought it. Isn't that right, Dad?" she asked, raising her voice.

"Mh?" said her dad. He shook his head. "I want to go home," he announced.

"You are home," said his daughter. "This is your new home, Dad. And very soon Mom will join you here." She turned to Franklin. "She's in the hospital right now, but we're hoping she'll be well enough soon so she can join Dad here at Edith Wale. It'll probably make things easier for him to settle in."

"What happened to the factory?" asked the woman's husband. "After you retired, I mean?"

"Oh, it's still there," said Franklin. "I never did manage to find a buyer for it. I suppose my son will sell the building and the land at some point. All of it belongs to him now." In actual fact, it belonged to the government, who had confiscated all of his assets but were dragging their feet in finding a new purpose for the land and the buildings. Probably they'd sell it to some developer.

"What happened to the stock of pet food?" asked the man, who seemed very interested.

"As far as I know it was auctioned off." Or maybe destroyed, as the FDA seemed insistent on.

NIC SAINT

The man held out his hand. "Dirk Lipscombe," he said. "An honor, sir."

He was touched by this and gave the man's hand a vigorous shake.

"And this is my wife Rebekka. And her dad Quinton, of course."

"I have a feeling you and Dad will get along great," said Rebekka.

She was the second person who had told him that by now, and he was starting to think that maybe it was true. "What business was your father in?" he asked.

"Construction," said Rebekka, and he remembered that Steven had mentioned this. "Mainly commercial real estate. Office buildings and such."

"Maybe he built that factory of yours, didn't you, Quinton?" Dirk quipped as he placed a hand on his father-in-law's shoulder. The man gave him a look of confusion, as if he couldn't quite place him.

"I doubt it," said Franklin. "We built that thing a long time ago—back in the stone ages when I was a young man," he added with a grin.

"Oh, but I think you and Dad are about the same age," said Rebekka. "How old are you, Franklin?"

"Um, seventy-four," he said.

"Same as Dad," she said.

"Do you have kids, Franklin?" asked Dirk.

"Yeah, two sons, who both used to work for the business. But like I said, neither of them was particularly interested in stepping into my shoes, so that was the end of that."

"Grandkids?"

"Two," he said. "My son Franklin Junior has two girls. Patsy and Tamara. They're still little," he said. "I married late and Franklin Junior also married late, otherwise I might have had great-grandkids by now." He decided not to mention that he hadn't seen the girls for years. They'd just feel sorry for him, and that was the last thing he needed. "Do you have kids?" Rebekka nodded, and Dirk took out his wallet and showed him two pictures of a couple of very rambunctious-looking boys. He smiled. "Great family," he said. "Congratulations."

"Thanks," said Rebekka. "It's not always easy to juggle work and home life, but we do our best."

"Listen, Franklin," said Dirk as he put a hand on his shoulder again and took him aside. "I don't know if you noticed, but Rebekka's dad is having some difficulties. You being his neighbor and all, could you maybe keep an eye on him? Nothing special, mind you. Just make him feel at home a little. Be a friend."

"Sure," he said. "Absolutely, Dirk." He felt honored that he'd ask.

"Thanks, Franklin," said Dirk. "It means a great deal to us." He locked eyes with him as his grip intensified, and he took Franklin's hand and pumped it eagerly. "A really great deal."

Franklin got the impression that there was more behind those words than simple gratitude for keeping an eye on a beloved father. But what it was, exactly, he did not know.

CHAPTER 26

Dooley had been right after all. That new portable AC unit Chase had purchased was a lifesaver of the first order. And so instead of spending my day in the basement glued to the floor and soaking up the last bit of coolness from the ground, I could simply lie on the couch and have a long nap without having to worry about my brain exploding in a burst of heat-induced fury. As long as I didn't go outside, for the world had been turned into a furnace once again.

Dooley was much braver than me, for he did venture outside from time to time, and each time he returned it was to deliver me the same message. "Don't go out there, Max—you'll melt!"

"I won't," I promised him. "I'll stay nice and cool inside."

Lucky for us, there was no need to go outside whatsoever, as our kibble was safely stored in that van located under the cover of a thick layer of shrubbery, which should also protect it from the worst of the heat. And since we're on the subject, it's probably useful to note that the four of us had held a meeting that morning and had decided that we were still going to go through with our plan of trying to salvage our kibble stash.

"Okay, so how much Plakka are we talking about here?" asked Harriet. "A minute amount, no doubt! So why should that stop us from enjoying our favorite kibble, you guys?"

"A sound argument if ever I heard one," said Brutus approvingly. "I'll bet that Uncle Alec, Chase, and Odelia were exaggerating. Probably this kibble doesn't contain any Plakka at all. These drug dealers simply tell people there's drugs in the stuff so they'll buy it. Something also known as the placebo effect. Isn't that right, Dooley?"

"Absolutely," said Dooley. "I've seen a documentary about that on the Discovery Channel, and the placebo effect is huge. In fact, it's bigger than huge. It's astronomical."

"See? Even science tells us that Franklin Cooper kibble is safe," said Brutus triumphantly.

And so it was decided. We wouldn't be swayed by these silly arguments Odelia had brought to bear on the whole discussion, and we would simply pursue our plan of making sure that we had enough kibble to last us a lifetime. And since I had already invited all of cat choir to partake in our stash, we couldn't back out now. They wouldn't understand specious arguments about narcotics and the like.

But as I lay there, enjoying my well-deserved and much-welcomed nap, suddenly a thought entered my head. And I shot up with a jerk. "The ants!" I cried.

"The ants?" asked Dooley. "What about the ants?"

"They'll eat our kibble!"

"No, they won't," said Brutus with a yawn. "For the simple fact that they don't know where it is." He gave me a look of suspicion. "Unless you told Lucian?"

"Of course I didn't tell Lucian," I said. "But I don't need to. Ants have an even better sense of smell than we do. They'll smell that kibble, and they'll confiscate it and feed it to their queen!"

"Oh, always with this queen," said Harriet. "As if she's the ruler of the whole world. It's not fair. Why does she get to have an army of soldiers collecting food for her and catering to her every whim while I have to do everything myself?"

Looks like someone was jealous, but despite my friend's assurances that our kibble was safe, I didn't get a moment's sleep from that moment on until the sun had finally set and had stopped turning the world into an oven. Dooley ventured outside a few more times before he gave us the all-clear, and we hurried over to the fence, hopped the thing, and landed on all fours in Blake's Field, en route to the police van we had stolen the night before. The moment we arrived, I saw that the worst had happened: the kibble was gone, with the last few nuggets being carted off by the army of ants under Lucian's command.

"You can't do this!" I cried, much dismayed.

"Do what?" asked Lucian innocently.

"You stole our kibble!" said Harriet. "Again!"

"Oh, this was your kibble, was it?" asked the ant leader. Or was it ant general? "Odd. I didn't see your name written on it."

"We brought that kibble here," said Brutus. "We stole it fair and square. Now give it back, you thief!"

Lucian put down the piece of kibble he had been carrying. "Okay, so let me get this straight. You stole this kibble, and now you're accusing me of stealing it from you? Doesn't that strike you as a little bit hypocritical?"

"No, it doesn't," I said. "It's still our kibble. And you took it."

Lucian shrugged. "My queen commands," he said. "And since she's a very demanding sort of queen, there's nothing I can do, fellows." And he was off with the last remaining piece of kibble.

"Oh, not again!" Harriet cried. "What is it about this queen that makes you do everything for her, Lucian? Can you explain it to me because I just don't get it."

Lucian thought for a moment. "There really isn't anything to explain," he said. "It's in our genetic makeup. Just like you like to prance around, Harriet. Or you like to stuff your face, Max. And you like to act tough, Brutus. Or the way you act all innocent, Dooley."

"It's not an act," I said. "Dooley really is that way."

"Well, so are we," said the ant. He gave me a wink. "When you deliver another batch of kibble, you will tell me, won't you, Max? My queen will be eternally grateful. She has told me that she's very fond of this particular type of kibble. In fact, she loves it."

"But so do we!" Dooley cried unhappily. "We adore that kibble!"

"Good to know," said Lucian and took off carrying his load.

"Hey, wait!" I said. "That kibble is poisoned, Lucian. It contains Plakka, which is a dangerous and highly addictive drug. If your queen eats too much of it, she will be in serious trouble."

"I don't believe you," said Lucian dryly. "You're just saying that to make me give you back your kibble. I'm sorry, Max, but I can see right through you."

"No, but it's true," said Harriet. "Our human is a cop, and he took this kibble to a lab, and they analyzed it, and it does contain Plakka. So you probably shouldn't eat it."

"And yet you couldn't wait to lay your paws on it. I call your bluff, Harriet."

I sighed deeply. "Okay, so maybe we're a little addicted to the stuff ourselves. Which is why we stole that police van last night and which is why we can't get enough of the stuff. But that's all the more reason for your queen not to eat it."

He cocked his head and eyed me closely with those facet eyes of his. Then he dumped the piece of kibble he had been carrying on the ground. "Here," he said. "You can have it, Max."

I stared at him. "What do you mean?"

"I'm giving this to you. As a token of appreciation for your assistance in feeding my queen." He took a step back and gestured to the piece of kibble. "Go on. Eat up."

I took in the piece of kibble, and I could feel a powerful pull inside of me practically force me to take him up on his offer. I resisted it with all of my might, but it was not to be. And so I jumped right on top of that piece of kibble and gobbled it up in a fraction of a second.

"Max!" said Harriet. "Haven't you ever heard of this thing called sharing?"

"I'm sorry!" I cried. "I couldn't resist!"

"Thanks for proving my point, Max," said Lucian. "Looks like that kibble is safe for feline consumption after all, or otherwise you wouldn't have eaten it. Adios, fellas!"

And with these words, he took off again.

"Wait!" I cried. "It's not safe to eat!"

"And yet you ate it, bud!" he yelled.

Darn it. Looked like I was an addict!

CHAPTER 27

After spending last night cruising the streets of Hampton Cove like a caped crusader—without the cape, mind you—Cliff Puckering felt the itch of going out there again. But when he told Mindy, she tut-tutted, "I wouldn't do that if I were you, Cliff."

"But why not? We did a lot of good things," he argued. "We got that gang of young punks arrested. We discovered a potential source of drugs. We stopped the dealers from putting more of their filth on the street..." He could have added that he'd seen four cats driving a police van, but since he'd promised Vesta that the topic was closed and he shouldn't mention it to anyone lest his invitation to be part of the watch was revoked, so he kept his tongue. Besides, it's not as if Mindy would believe it. He hardly believed it himself. But then such was the life of a watch member: full of excitement and action!

"Look, I don't think it's safe," said Mindy. "And I was hoping that now that you went out there and joined those crazy ladies you got that out of your system and wouldn't have to do it again. But clearly, you're enamored with one of them, or maybe both of them," she concluded as she picked up her needlework and continued creating another little masterpiece for one of their granddaughters.

"Enamored! Me! At my age!"

She pursed her lips. "Don't think I haven't noticed how you can't stop talking about them, especially that Scarlett Canyon. And we both know what kind of woman she is."

"And what kind is that?" he asked, very much amused by these accusations.

"It's all in the name, Cliff. Scarlett Canyon is a scarlet woman," she snapped. "Going out with a different man every week. I've seen her at the senior center, and I know her reputation. She dated pretty much every single male there, but that hasn't stopped her from hitting on you, I imagine."

"She hasn't been hitting on me! She's not even interested in me whatsoever. And I'm not interested in her. I just feel…"

"Yes?" she said, giving him a critical look. "Physically attracted? She is a very attractive woman, Cliff, I'll give you that. But to throw your wedding vows in the trash after fifty years of marriage for some loosey-goosey freakiness with a woman like that?" She pursed her lips. "Frankly, I'm disappointed. Extremely disappointed. And that's what I told Lily."

"You told our daughter that I'm having an affair with Scarlett Canyon?"

"Absolutely. She has a right to know. After the mess Rick made of things, she's extra-sensitive about these things."

Lily and Rick had recently decided to take a break from their marriage after Rick had been unfaithful to his wife with his yoga teacher—a very bendy woman twenty years his junior. No one understood what had gotten into the man to throw away a wonderful marriage that had given them two amazing daughters, but then Rick had never been the brightest bulb.

"Look, I can promise you right now that there's absolutely nothing going on between me and Scarlett," he said. "In fact..." He bit his lip.

She gazed up above her half-moon reading glasses. "In fact?" she prompted.

"In fact, I'm not sure I like her very much. I mean, she and Vesta do seem to take an awful lot of risks. Risks that, frankly, I'm not sure I can condone. Take last night, for instance. They practically got us all killed with their antics." It was exciting, of course, the stuff you only saw on television in one of those action movies. But it was also dangerous. And now he wondered if it was *too* dangerous. He couldn't wait to get out there again, of course, but was this adrenaline shot he'd gotten last night too much of a good thing? Was he going to get himself killed in the process? And was it all worth it?

"Look, you do what you need to do, of course," said Mindy airily. "And far be it from me to stop you from going out there again. But I can tell you right now that I don't like it."

No, he could definitely see that, but whether it was the Scarlett thing or simply because Mindy foresaw some dangerous situation getting out of hand and getting her husband killed was difficult to determine. Maybe a little bit of both.

And so when Vesta gave him a call on his mobile ten minutes later and told him to be ready at the door and she would pick him up, he hesitated. "Maybe I should sit this one out," he said, as he darted a look at his intractable wife. He didn't want to lose his marriage over his ambition to play cops and robbers.

"What are you talking about?" said Vesta. "I thought you couldn't wait to get out there again? To be part of the watch?"

"I know," he said, as he walked into the kitchen and

lowered his voice. "The thing is that Mindy isn't as keen as I would have liked. She thinks…"

"She thinks what?" asked Vesta.

He glanced at the door, and lowered his voice even more. "She thinks I'm having an affair with Scarlett."

The raucous jolliment that hit his eardrum was testament to Vesta's sentiments about this particular suspicion. "An affair! You and Scarlett! This must be some kind of joke!"

He should have felt insulted, but truth be told, he figured she was probably right to laugh it off. Scarlett was quite obviously out of his league and he knew it. Too bad that Mindy didn't. On the other hand, it was kind of flattering that she would still be jealous of other women, after having been married to him for five decades.

"Okay, if it makes you feel any better, Scarlett can't join us tonight. So it's just me and you and Francis."

"Francis, really?" he asked, bucking up considerably. He couldn't imagine the gray-haired priest getting into all manner of mayhem. He seemed the soul of discretion and common sense.

"So are you in or are you out?" asked Vesta.

"I'm in," he said determinedly. Mindy couldn't possibly have any objections to him going on patrol with the likes of Francis Reilly, seeing as he was their priest of long standing.

"Great. I'll pick you up at ten."

"Anything special on the program tonight?" he asked.

"I think you'll find that we'll probably have a very peaceful night," she said, much to his relief, though also to his slight disappointment. "That's the way with the neighborhood watch: mostly, it's just cruising around and nothing happens. Like I told you, last night was an exception. So better pack something to eat and a hot flask of tea." And with these words, she disconnected, and he eagerly joined his wife in the living room to give her the good news that he'd be keeping Hampton Cove safe tonight in the company of none other than Francis Reilly.

As he had expected, she was much relieved and even gave him her full blessing. What he hadn't expected, though, was that she had another suggestion, and it was non-negotiable: she was going to join him on tonight's patrol.

"But Mindy!" he said. "I thought you didn't like the watch? That it was far too dangerous?"

"I know, but I want to see what you're up to on these patrols, and the only way to do it is by signing up as well." She gave him a cheerful smile. "Aren't you pleased? We'll be riding together—husband and wife—just as God intended."

He didn't know if God ever intended couples to go on neighborhood watch patrol together, but then there was probably a lot that he didn't know about the Big Man's intentions. What he did know was that he could hardly say no. Secretly he thought that she simply wanted to check if it was really true that Scarlett wouldn't be joining them that night. And maybe it was for the best. She would definitely discover there wasn't anything untoward going on.

So finally he nodded. "Okay, fine. I'll tell Vesta. But be warned that things might get very boring. Mostly watch business is just driving around and looking at deserted streets and checking on people doing absolutely nothing out of the ordinary."

"Great!" she said happily as she put down her needlework.

"Great," he said. Oh, dear. What had he gotten them into?

CHAPTER 28

We had decided to opt out of joining Gran on her nocturnal patrol since we had more important things to do. And since she hadn't really been instrumental in us retrieving our kibble—the ants had thwarted that particular plan—we didn't feel we were beholden to her. And so the four of us headed to the park, where cat choir likes to rehearse. Only our destination wasn't cat choir, per se, but a different endeavor altogether. After I had made the startling discovery that I was, in fact, a kibble addict, my friends had grudgingly come to the same conclusion, and since we felt we needed to address the subject, Harriet had come up with the bright idea to launch our very own—and possibly the world's first—twelve-step program for cats.

And so we selected a nice spot near the beach for our inaugural meeting, and Harriet took the floor. "We are all gathered here to launch our first twelve-step group for cat addicts," she said.

"Not for people addicted to cats, though," Brutus amended.

"No, not for people addicted to cats," she agreed. "But for cats addicted to something. Whether it be kibble or wet food pouches or catnip..."

"Can cats become addicted to catnip?" asked Dooley.

"Absolutely," said Harriet. "Just like any substance, catnip can have an addictive effect. Just like there are humans that are addicted to glue, for instance, or cough syrup or fluorescent markers, cats can be addicted to catnip. Why, are you addicted to catnip, Dooley? Don't hold back. This is a safe space, and we're all in the same boat here." She eyed him expectantly.

"I don't *think* I'm addicted to catnip," said our friend thoughtfully. "I mean, do I like it? Sure. But can I do without?" He hesitated. "I think so? I mean, they put it in everything these days, don't they? So it's very hard to be without it."

"Dooley is right," Brutus said, nodding. "Like they put sugar in human food, they put catnip in cat food. Overdoing it a little, if you ask me."

We looked up when two more cats approached. They were Kingman and Shanille. Much surprised, Harriet asked, "Don't you have to direct cat choir, Shanille?"

"I heard about your new group," said our choir leader. "And I didn't want to miss it for the world. Which is why I decided to suspend cat choir for one night." She shrugged. "It's not as if they're going to miss the rehearsal. As we all know that's just an excuse to get together and have a gossipfest."

We shared a look of surprise. Everyone knew that cat choir wasn't exactly on everyone's list because of its musical qualities, but to hear Shanille admit it was something else. And before long, more cats walked up to join our meeting. Amongst them was Clarice, of course, Scarlett's cat, but also our good friends Buster, Tom, Tigger, Misty, Shadow, Missy,

NIC SAINT

Samantha and many others. All in all, it looked as if more cats had a problem with addiction than we would have thought. And after a lot of back and forth, mainly connected with the articles of association and administrative and frankly tedious aspects of launching a new organization, I finally decided that I wanted to address the gathering and share some of my personal concerns. And so I stepped to the fore and introduced myself.

"Hi, I'm Max," I said. "And I'm an addict."

"Hi, Max!" said the gathering.

"It's been one hour and thirty minutes since I've last eaten Franklin Cooper kibble, and even though I knew full well that it contained a substance that might be bad for me, I still couldn't resist the urge to eat it." I hung my head in shame, but my friends weren't having any of that nonsense.

"Don't feel bad, Max," said Kingman. "I've eaten a lot worse than that Franklin Cooper junk, and even though I knew exactly what it was I was putting in my body, I still went ahead and did it."

"I once ate a piece of chocolate," Shanille confessed. "Even though I knew I shouldn't."

"But you shouldn't, Shanille," said Buster.

"I know, Buster," Shanille snapped. "I said I shouldn't, didn't I?"

"No judgment, please," said Harriet, holding up her paws. "We're here to help and support each other, not to cast aspersions."

"Understood," said Buster. "And it's true that I've eaten chocolate, too. I felt really sick afterward, and Fido even had to take me to the vet, and Vena had to pump my stomach. And even then, I still wanted to have another piece. So I guess I'm a chocoholic, you guys."

"I once ate a shoe," said Clarice. "It wasn't even delicious, but there was something about it that kept me going back for seconds. Tough to chew, though—especially the sole. I think it may have been rubber."

For a moment, no one spoke, then all of those present started talking simultaneously.

"I once ate a feather," said Tigger, the plumber's cat.

"I once ate a tennis ball," said Misty, the electrician's cat.

"I once ate a sponge," said Missy, the landscaper's cat.

"I once ate my human's finger," said Shadow, who belongs to the guy that runs the hardware store. "Well, to be fair, I only had a nibble before he stopped me. I guess humans don't like to be nibbled at. They're very particular about it."

Turns out we all had a story of addiction to tell, and were relieved finally to be able to tell it. But since Harriet likes an orderly meeting, she reiterated some ground rules, namely that only one cat at a time should have the floor. And so our first meeting proceeded, and I have to say it was quite the eye-opener.

"Hi, I'm Dooley," I said Dooley. "And I'm an addict."

"Hi, Dooley!" cried all the rest of the cats.

"It's been three days since I last chewed Odelia's computer cable."

"Dooley?" I said. "I thought Odelia said you shouldn't?"

"I know!" he wailed. "But I can't help it. It's stronger than myself!"

"You could get an electric shock," I added, but when Harriet gave me a stern look and reminded me of the 'no judgment' rule, I immediately shut up. She was right. Who was I to judge my friend for nibbling on a computer cable when I couldn't stop thinking about Franklin Cooper kibble, which was probably even worse for me than a nice cable, which probably is full of fiber and other fine nutrients?

By the time the meeting ended, I think all of those present felt they had gone through a transformational experience. And since part of the twelve-step program is to have a buddy,

Harriet assigned Dooley to me as my buddy, and vice versa. Which was great, since we live together anyway, so we could always talk to each other when we were going through a tough time.

Walking home, I have to say I felt a lot lighter. I knew that I'd still find temptation crossing my path, but with my friends by my side, maybe I would be able to resist it—one day at a time. Though in actual fact, it wouldn't be that hard, since our last bags of kibble had been stolen—by Lucian and his colony. Which reminded me: "Maybe we should start a group for ants? They seem to be addicted to that kibble too."

"I'm afraid that would be taking things too far," said Harriet with a smile. "And besides, the first step to solving a problem is admitting that you have a problem, Max. And clearly Lucian and his queen are not at that stage yet."

"No, I guess they aren't," I said.

She sighed happily. "Well, that was fun, wasn't it?"

Fun wasn't the word I would have used, but it was true that it had been a great experience for all.

"Now if only we can start these groups in every city in the country, I think we're well on our way to putting mental health for cats on the map, you guys."

I gave her a look of alarm. "You want to start these groups all over the country?"

"Of course. We shouldn't keep this to ourselves. Everyone will benefit. And as we all know, plenty of celebrities suffer from addiction problems and join these groups. I mean, you could almost say that these AA-type meetings have become the go-to networking events for the stars of this world. Used to be that you had to go to some Hollywood party to mix and mingle, but nowadays it's a much better use of your time to visit your local AA meeting."

"I'm not sure that's actually the case," I said carefully.

"Oh, but I'm sure it's true," said Harriet. "So once I've put this cat AA business on the map, I'm sure we'll start to see some stars attend our meetings. And that's how you get the ball rolling. Before you know it, we'll be offered movie parts or stage a Broadway play. The celebrity life awaits us, you guys, and frankly I can't wait until it finally happens!"

I could have told her that humans probably wouldn't come to our meetings, but then she was so convinced of the bright future that awaited her I didn't have the heart to burst her bubble. Which is when Dooley addressed another valid point.

"What are we going to call ourselves?" he asked. "We can't call ourselves the CAA, can we? Cat Anonymous Alcoholics doesn't really seem to capture what we're trying to do here."

"No, CAA doesn't seem to fit the bill," Harriet agreed thoughtfully. Then she brightened. "How about AAC? Anonymous Alcoholic Cats? Though we're not actually alcoholics, are we?"

"No, we're kibble-oholics," I said.

"I'm an electric cable-oholic," said Dooley.

"And I'm a catnip-oholic," Brutus confessed.

"And I'm a star!" said Harriet as she lifted her gaze to the heavens and spread her paws. Then she realized this wasn't exactly pertinent, and when Dooley suggested she might be a celebrity-oholic or even a star-oholic, she seemed disgruntled. "Okay, so let's just say we're all addicted to something," she said. "Doesn't matter what. So how about Caddicts Anonymous?"

"We're not very anonymous, though," I pointed out. "By now we know about every one of our friends' addictions since all the cats of Hampton Cove were there, and I'm sure tomorrow the only topic of conversation will be the different substances we're all addicted to." I guess cats don't have the same qualms humans have about keeping their addictions private. "So how about simply calling ourselves Caddicts? You know, short for cat addicts?"

"Caddicts, it is," said Harriet. "And can I just say how proud I am of all of you? You really held nothing back, and that's what's going to turn this new venture of ours into a resounding success." Her eyes sparkled. "Very soon now we'll be on the front page of every newspaper and being interviewed on every talk show. Then there will be Caddicts the Stage Play, Caddicts the Musical, and finally Caddicts the Movie, in which I will star, of course."

"Of course," I murmured.

"Can I also be in your movie, Harriet?" asked Dooley.

"Of course, Dooley," said Harriet magnanimously. "In fact, you can all be in my movie. As long as you understand that I will take first billing. After all, there can only be one star." She pressed her front paws to her chest and threw her head back dramatically. *"Moi!"*

CHAPTER 29

Vesta wasn't sure what to think of all of these newcomers. Yesterday Cliff had hitched a ride with them, and now his wife had insisted to sign up for their patrols. But since she was essentially a generous and kind-hearted sort of person, she decided to give these wannabe watch members a chance. After all, Cliff had behaved exemplarily last night, and so maybe his wife would be cut from the same cloth. Unfortunately for them, not much seemed to be happening, and so after they had been driving around for what felt like half the night, Mindy asked, "Is this the way it always goes?"

"Well, mostly so," she admitted. "Though sometimes we do get into some action involving the criminal element. But tonight seems an especially slow night."

"And a good thing, too!" said Francis. "In fact, I think we should all strive for nights exactly like these, when the good people of Hampton Cove are all asleep peacefully in their beds, and no burglaries are taking place, and no crimes are being committed. Then we'll know that the watch has made a difference in people's lives. Wouldn't you agree, Vesta?"

"Oh, absolutely," she said. Though truth be told, she preferred when there was at least some action involved. Not like last night—that had been excessive, even for her standards. But a little bit of activity would have been welcome to break the monotony and the tedium. And since there didn't seem to be a lot happening in town, she had directed her old car to the outskirts.

"Is your car fine now?" asked Cliff from the backseat. "I thought it was broken?"

"Well, it was," she said. "Something to do with the engine. But I took it to the garage today, and they got it fixed in a jiffy." She didn't mention that it was actually her daughter Marge's car and that she hadn't dared tell her about the damage it had sustained, so she had asked one of her friends from the senior center to take a look, and the retired mechanic had fixed things for a dance with her at the next senior center dance, which wouldn't exactly be a hardship since he was a catch, even at eighty-seven. And she always adored an older man. They were so much more experienced, after all.

They were now traversing what was commonly known as the canal zone, since it was located near the canal, and mostly featured factories and businesses that flocked there.

"Isn't this where the old Franklin Cooper factory used to be?" asked Francis.

"Yeah, it should be around here somewhere," said Mindy, scooting forward a little and poking her head between the two seats to take a better look. "I used to work there, you see," she explained. "Well, both of us did—isn't that so, Cliff?"

She didn't seem as suspicious of her husband having an affair with Scarlett as she was before and even seemed excited to be on patrol with them.

"I didn't know you both used to work at Franklin Cooper," said Gran.

PURRFECT KIBBLE

"For our sins, yeah," Cliff quipped. "Long time ago now. Back when the factory was still thriving."

"The golden days," said Mindy. "When Mr. Cooper Senior was in charge. The moment his son took over, things quickly went south. But then that was after our time."

"We still keep in touch with some of the former colleagues, though," said Cliff. "And they told us all about the way Franklin Junior destroyed his father's company by making some dubious business decisions."

"If it's true that their kibble was stuffed with Plakka, those decisions weren't just dubious but downright criminal," said Francis.

"Yeah, Franklin Senior would never have done such a thing," said Mindy. "He was an honest and frankly brilliant businessman, who managed to make us the number one pet food in the country."

"There it is," said Cliff as he pointed along a narrow side street. "I can see the entrance from here."

"That's where we met, Cliff and I," said Mindy. "When we got married, we even got a wedding present from Mr. Cooper himself."

"And a nice bonus," said Cliff, nodding. "To buy ourselves a house, he said. Though of course, the bonus wasn't as big as all that, but it's the gesture that counts."

"He was a good man," said Mindy. "I wonder what became of him."

"He's at Edith Wale," said Francis. "I paid him a visit there once, but he wasn't the man he used to be. Very bitter. And his sons weren't speaking to him anymore. I believe Franklin Junior even took out a court order so his father couldn't see his granddaughters anymore, which I felt was simply cruel."

"Oh, that's horrible," said Mindy. "But why?"

"Franklin Junior is a spiteful little man," said Cliff. "He probably blamed his dad for what happened, since most likely he was the one who blew the whistle on those illegal practices."

"You think that Franklin Senior was behind that FDA raid?" asked Mindy.

"That's the rumor that's been doing the rounds for a while now."

"Such a shame," said Mindy, shaking her head.

They had reached the entrance to the old factory, and even though the gates were closed, they could see the silhouette of the buildings behind it, and it was obvious that it had been a pretty impressive operation. And as Vesta parked the car in front of it so they could have a closer look, suddenly she thought she saw lights flashing inside those old buildings.

"There's someone there," she said.

"You're right," said Mindy.

And since they were the watch, and curiosity was her second name, they all got out of the car and the four of them made their way to the entrance and peered through the gate for a closer look.

"There are vans parked there," said Mindy.

"I thought this place was deserted," said Francis.

"Obviously there's some activity still going on," said Cliff.

For a moment, they simply watched on, then Vesta said, "Let's go and have a closer look."

"But it's private property," said Mindy. "We can't trespass on private property, can we?"

She gave the woman an indulgent smile. "We're the watch, Mindy. We can trespass on anything."

Lucky for them, the iron gates were open, so all they had to do was pass through and they were in. And as they approached the vans, she saw that several men were loading boxes into those vans. "I'm having déjà vu," she said. "Tell me

I'm wrong, but doesn't that look like boxes of kibble being loaded?"

"By golly, you're right," said Cliff. "Just like last night. I even recognize that guy over there. It's the same bruiser we saw last night." He cut a nervous look at Vesta. "We should probably call the cops. These men are looting the place."

"Not so quick," she said. "Let's find out what's going on first, shall we?"

Mindy chewed her lower lip. "I know how we can get past those goons."

"Mindy, no," said Cliff. "We're not the police. We might get hurt."

"Oh, don't be such a ninny," said the woman, much to Vesta's surprise. She beckoned the rest of them. "Follow me," she said. And before they could stop her, she was off.

Looked like Vesta had been wrong. Mindy was a born watch member!

CHAPTER 30

It didn't take Mindy long to lead her fellow watch members into the factory through a well-hidden side entrance that she claimed had mainly been used by the workers to have a quick smoke without any of the foremen catching them, and then they found themselves on the factory floor. The machines that had been used in the production of the fabled kibble were still there, and also the production lines.

"Oh, does this bring back memories," said Mindy.

"It sure does," said Cliff as both of the pensioners gazed fondly at the impressive installations. It surprised Vesta that it wouldn't have been dismantled and sold for parts in the time that had passed between the FDA raid that had closed down the factory and now, since it had been a few years.

"We better get out of here," Francis urged. The priest didn't look entirely at ease sneaking around the factory in the middle of the night.

"Let's first see what's going on," Vesta suggested. She had called the cops before when coming upon the scene of what she and Scarlett believed to be a crime in progress, only to be rebuffed when everything had been on the up and up. It made the watch look like fools, and she wanted to avoid that. She snuck along the wall in the direction of the loading docks, where all the activity seemed to be taking place. Loud voices alerted her to the fact that they were close, and as they peeked around the corner, she saw that a mountain of the same kibble had been piled up near one of the loading bays, and it was being transferred into those waiting vans by half a dozen men, a couple of whom she recognized from the night before.

"Looks like it's the same gang," she whispered. "The ones responsible for that dead body that was found."

"A dead body?" asked Mindy. "Cliff, you didn't mention a dead body!"

"I didn't want to scare you," said Cliff.

"What dead body?" asked Francis, who was as clueless as Mindy.

"According to the police, he was a robber," Vesta explained. "And his death was an accident. Self-defense."

"Who killed him?" asked Mindy.

"Do you know the toy store on Main Street? It's run by a gun named Felix? Felix Bennett?"

"Oh, no!" she said. "I always go there to buy presents for my grandkids."

"Well, that's the one," she said. "But like I said, it was an accident, or so Felix claims." Though as far as she had been able to ascertain from things Chase had told her, he hadn't lied. Why a blond-haired customer would have offered to assist him in getting rid of the body was a little less clear. And how the body had ended up in that old house on Alhola Street, along with Felix himself, even less so. But then that wasn't Vesta's concern but Chase's.

"Okay, I think I've seen enough," she said, and was about to quietly retreat and go back the way they had come so they could call the police, when a large man blocked their progress. Much to her chagrin, he was holding up a gun and was pointing it at them. And if the frown on his ugly mug was any indication, she got the distinct impression he wouldn't be afraid to use it.

* * *

Franklin Cooper woke up in the middle of the night to find that a man was standing over him holding a pillow in his hands. "You're in my room," the man said, and then pressed the pillow down over his head. Lucky for Franklin, who discovered that it's hard to breathe when someone is pushing a pillow down over your face, he always kept a flashlight under his own pillow, as he had a habit of having to go to the bathroom several times a night, and also found himself a little unsteady on his feet lately. So he grabbed the flashlight and swung it wildly at what he thought was the other man's head.

It must have connected, for the pressure on the pillow eased, and finally, he could breathe again. And as he turned on the flashlight and shone it at the man, he saw that he was lying on the ground, out for the count. He grabbed his glasses from the bedside table and put them on.

It was only then that he realized that the man who had just tried to kill him was his new neighbor, Quinton Banyard.

"Christ," he muttered, and immediately pressed the alarm button located next to his bed. Within minutes, Steven came hurrying in, and when he saw the man on the floor, calmly turned to Franklin.

"Now what did you do?"

"He attacked me!" said Franklin. "I woke up, and he was

standing there with that pillow, and then he pressed it down on my face. I couldn't breathe!"

Steven frowned and knelt down next to the man, pressing his index finger against his neck to feel for a pulse. "He's all right," he said. "Just unconscious."

"Oh, thank God," said Franklin. The last thing he needed was to have a murder charge hanging over his head. "I don't know what got into him. He said, 'You're in my room,' and then put that pillow on my face. I thought I was a goner, for sure."

"He must have been confused," said Steven. "Thought that this was his room and that you were an intruder." He had placed his phone to his ear, and when the call connected, arranged for an ambulance so the unconscious man could be taken to the hospital.

Franklin realized that he'd been very lucky. If that flashlight hadn't been concealed under his pillow, he would never have had the strength to fight off this guy, who was a lot stronger than he looked, and had pressed that pillow down with considerable strength.

"I'll notify his family," said Steven. "And the police. We can't have this sort of thing going on here. And if the police investigation bears out your story, he'll simply have to go."

"Yeah, I guess it's not a good idea to keep him here," Franklin agreed wholeheartedly.

"Are you all right?" asked the orderly, and did a couple of checks to make sure that he hadn't suffered any adverse consequences from the episode.

"I'm fine," he said, waving the man away. "Good thing I keep a flashlight under my pillow, or you would have found a corpse lying in my bed tomorrow morning."

Steven smiled. "I'm sorry this happened to you, Franklin. Will you be all right staying here tonight, or do you want me to assign you another room for the time being?"

"No, I'm fine," he said. "Just... get this guy out of here, will you?"

Steven nodded. "Once the ambulance gets here, and the police, we'll leave you in peace."

And since he had a feeling that might take a while, he suddenly got a powerful urge to talk to someone about what had just happened to him. Life is fleeting, and never had it borne in on him more than it had in these past few minutes. And so he grabbed his phone and called up a familiar number.

"Dad?" asked a groggy-sounding Franklin Jr. "It's the middle of the night."

"Someone tried to kill me," he said curtly, not seeing a need to beat about the bush.

"What? What are you talking about?"

"My new neighbor," he said. "He tried to murder me by pressing a pillow over my head just now." And he explained to his son, whom he hadn't spoken to in months, what had happened.

Much to Franklin Jr.'s credit, he said, "I'm coming down there."

"But..."

"No buts. I'll be there in ten minutes."

It wasn't what he'd expected, but it certainly was what he'd hoped. And as he put the phone down, he saw that his hand was shaking. Obviously he wasn't as fine as he'd told Steven.

CHAPTER 31

The next morning, bright and early, I awoke feeling much refreshed and happy. I knew that the Franklin Cooper kibble was not of this world anymore, and that the last bags had been confiscated by Lucian to be delivered to his queen, and so never again would I be tempted to give in to my addiction. I felt a powerful urge to share my newfound happiness.

"Do you know what day is today?" I asked Dooley, who was lying next to me at the foot of the bed of our humans.

"Um... Tuesday?" he ventured.

"Today is the second day I haven't eaten Franklin Cooper kibble," I said. "Oh, happy day!"

He thought for a moment, then he got why this made me so happy. "Today is the third day I haven't chewed on any of Odelia's computer cables," he announced. "Though I did chew on her phone cable yesterday, but that probably doesn't count, does it?"

I smiled. "A cable is a cable, Dooley. And I think you should probably refrain from chewing on either of those."

"Yeah, I guess you're right," he said. "Good thing we have

Caddicts now. Do you think we'll meet regularly from now on?"

"I'm sure we will," I said. Though I didn't see the point in me having to attend, as the object of my addiction was being masticated by an ant queen as we spoke, I still felt I should support my fellow cats in their battle against addiction.

Odelia stretched and then lifted her head to gaze down at us. "So what have you been up to last night?"

"Oh, nothing special," I said.

"We had the first inaugural meeting of Caddicts," said Dooley. "And Harriet is our president."

"Caddicts? What is Caddicts?"

"It's a twelve-step program for cats," I explained.

"I didn't know cats could be addicted," she said.

"Oh, sure we can," I said. "For instance…"

"You don't have to tell me," she said, holding up a hand. "It's called Addicts Anonymous for a reason. What goes on in the meeting stays in the meeting."

I could have told her that this wasn't how cats handled things, and that what had gone on in the last meeting would be all over town today, but I had a feeling she had other fish to fry. And besides, I didn't really want to tell her about my addiction. There are some things that a cat likes to keep to himself.

Odelia got out of bed and checked on Grace, who was already awake and gazing down at us from her cot. Once she had ascertained that her daughter was fine, she disappeared into the bathroom.

"Oh, before I forget," said Dooley, "there was something we wanted to ask you, Gracey."

"What's that?" asked the little girl.

"You remember how we used to love that Franklin Cooper kibble so much? Well, we stole a police car full of the stuff two nights ago, and parked it in Blake's Field. But we still need someone to help us unload the van and take the kibble to Tex's garden house."

"Dooley!" I said. "The kibble is gone, remember?"

My friend blinked a few times, then a smile spread across his features. "Oh, my God! Of course! Never mind, Grace. It was something I had put on my to-do list before I forgot I didn't have to do it anymore."

"I want to help," said Grace. "Just tell me what it is you want me to do and I'll do it."

"We were going to ask you to help us transport that kibble to Tex's garden house," I explained. "But since it's gone now, there's no need."

"That's too bad," said Grace. "Though I'm not sure I would have been able to drag bags of kibble from one place to the other, and climb a fence in the process. I mean, I may be a lot of things but I'm not Supergirl, you know."

We both smiled. "No, I guess you're not," I said. Though we certainly like to think of her as Supergirl.

"We were going to ask if you could get your daycare friends to chip in," Dooley explained. "But now of course that's no longer necessary."

"It's a good idea," she agreed. "We could use a joint project, as the other kids sometimes seem a little impassive to my taste. A nice big project could get them out of their stupor."

I couldn't imagine any kids being impassive, but then I guess to a hyperactive kid like Grace, any kid that isn't as active as she is comes across as impassive. I was glad now that I hadn't asked her to go ahead with this, as those kids' parents probably would have frowned upon their offspring running amok and transferring boxes of kibble from one place to the next. Invariably it would have gotten out somehow, and then we would have gotten the blame.

NIC SAINT

In other words, nothing but good things were happening to me that day!

And it was with a happy feeling of possibility that I jumped down from the bed, ready to start my day. I had only just arrived in the kitchen when Marge came hurrying in. "Have you seen Ma?" she asked urgently.

"No, I haven't," said Odelia, who was busy popping a capsule into the coffee machine.

"She didn't come home last night," said Marge. "And she's not answering her phone."

"Have you asked Scarlett? Maybe they're still on patrol? You know how those two get when they're busy with their neighborhood watch."

"Good idea," said Marge, and took out her phone. Moments later she was in communication with Scarlett. "What do you mean you didn't go on patrol last night?" she practically screamed. "A date? You have got to be kidding! So where's my mother?!"

When she hung up, she looked even more worried than before. "Scarlett says that she had a date last night, so she didn't go patrolling with the others."

"The others?" asked Odelia.

"Yeah, Francis Reilly was going, and also the new guy. Cliff something, and his wife Mindy."

"Oh, I think I met them," said Odelia. "They were at the house where we found that dead man. Call Francis," she said. "He'll know where they are. Probably still out on patrol, like I said."

But Father Reilly's phone also went straight to voicemail, and that wasn't something that made Marge feel more relaxed about what could have happened to Gran. Quite the contrary. And so the next phone call was to her brother, and hopefully he could shed some light on Gran's whereabouts.

Maybe she had been arrested again, as often seems to happen.

So when Uncle Alec assured her that everything was fine but also admitted that he had absolutely no idea where Gran could be, Marge actually burst into tears—one of the first times I'd ever seen her cry. I have to say it wasn't a sight that allowed me to sustain my very good mood. On the contrary. Suddenly I felt a powerful urge to have another nibble at that very fine Franklin Cooper kibble.

CHAPTER 32

"This is one right mess," Rebekka grumbled as she paced her office. First, her dad tried to murder a resident at his new nursing home, and now one of the workers at the old Franklin Cooper factory announced they had caught four pensioners sneaking around and had locked them up, just to be on the safe side. "Can't these people do anything right?"

"They were sneaking around, sis," said her brother Daavid as he regarded her closely.

"So what? They were probably part of one of those urban explorer groups that are all the rage," she said. "Or maybe they got lost on their way back to the tour bus after a day at the beach."

"They're all part of the same neighborhood watch group," said her other brother Aappo.

"Neighborhood watch? So what were they doing at the factory?"

"Two of them used to work there," said Daavid. "So maybe they wanted to relive their glory days? Or give their friends a tour of the facility?"

"What do you want us to do with them?" asked Aappo, cracking his knuckles, a habit she abhorred and had hated ever since they were kids together.

"What did they see?"

"They were caught spying on our operation. So they probably saw enough to cause us some serious problems if we let them walk. Oh, and one of them is the chief of police's mother."

She threw up her hands. "Oh, for crying out loud!"

"And the fourth member of the party is a priest," said Aappo with a grin. He had always enjoyed seeing her, their big sister, in distress. Ever since she had taken over the family reins from their dad, they had been eager to see her make a fool of herself so they could take over. But that wasn't going to happen. She just needed to think. "We were never going to be able to use that place anyway," she said. "Too conspicuous. How hard would it be to take that equipment and install it somewhere else?"

"We're talking tons of machinery," said Daavid, who quickly caught her drift. Whereas Aappo was more the muscles in their outfit, Daavid at least had inherited some of their dad's brains. Though it now looked as if Dad had lost his capacity for straight thinking altogether, or else he wouldn't have attacked that poor guy in his nursing home for thinking he was an intruder. "But I guess it could be done. Maybe a week? Two weeks, tops?"

"Okay, do it," she said with the decisiveness that had always been her strong suit.

"Where do you want us to take it?"

"Let's just store it at the villa for now," she suggested. "We can scout for a new location as soon as this whole thing blows over. And make sure you tell your goons to treat the prisoners with respect. We don't want the chief's mother to get worked over by some overzealous idiot."

Aappo stiffened. "My men aren't idiots," he said.

"Says you."

He would have shrugged if he'd had a neck that was separate from his shoulders. She could never understand why anyone would want to turn himself into a cartoon character, but obviously Aappo derived a certain enjoyment from spending all of his leisure time pumping iron at the gym. It certainly didn't hurt his standing with his men, who were all cut from the same cloth.

"Where are they now?"

"Still at the factory," said Daavid curtly. "We figured it was too risky to move them."

"Good thinking," she said, giving her brother a rare compliment. "But you better get them out of there before someone comes looking. Put them up at the Alhola Street place."

Both her brothers stared at her as if she'd lost her mind. "But that house was raided!" said Frank.

"So? That means it's the last place the police will look. And make sure they don't escape, for that would jeopardize a million-dollar operation and is the last thing we need."

Both men nodded, and Aappo left to give his goons the necessary instructions. Daavid stayed behind and gave her an odd look. "So what about Dad?"

"They won't charge him with attempted murder," she said. "It's obvious he's not in a good way. They'll probably have him admitted to a mental health facility, which probably is a good idea anyway."

"But what about Mom? She can't stay with him in that facility, surely?"

"No, I guess not," she said. But since she didn't immediately see a solution, she dismissed her brother and told him they'd have to talk about it some other time since she was busy.

Twenty minutes later, she was taking her sons to school and wondering what to do about her mom and dad. It certainly wasn't the kind of thing any daughter liked to tell their parent: that Dad had tried to murder an innocent man in his bed. Then again, maybe they shouldn't tell Mom. She wasn't in a good place as it was, and this might tip her over the edge.

She dropped the boys off at school and drove on to the police station, where they had taken Dad after he had been arrested last night. Knowing Chief Lip, he wouldn't make things difficult for them and wouldn't insist on keeping Dad locked up any longer than was strictly necessary. Even though he was a cop, he was a good man, with his heart in the right place.

Which is when she happened to see a familiar figure crossing the road. It was Freddie Tottman. And in spite of her erstwhile desire to make the man pay for the trouble he'd caused, she realized she would probably be better served by making amends and putting the episode behind her. She simply didn't have the bandwidth to deal with the annoying little twerp. A simple matter of energy allocation.

So she parked the car and grabbed her blond wig from the glove compartment.

CHAPTER 33

Freddie had finished his first shift at the bakery and decided to take a break by eating his croissant in the small park in front of Town Hall, located around the block from the bakery. After the shocking events of the past couple of days, his boss had told him he could take as much time off as he needed to, but he had said he wanted to go back to work as soon as possible, since sitting at home would make things even more difficult for him, just reliving that awful night in captivity, fearing for his life. And as he took the croissant out of the paper bag and took a sip from the cup of delicious sweet coffee, he didn't look up when a woman sat down next to him.

"That looks tasty," she said.

"It is," he assured her. "And I should know, since I made it myself."

"Oh, so you're a baker, are you… Freddie?"

A chill ran along his spine as he slowly turned his head to take in the woman. It was as he had feared: the same woman he'd run into several times now, and who had been instrumental in locking him up.

"You," he said.

She gave him a frosty smile. "We keep bumping into each other, don't we, Freddie?"

"I don't think I've had the benefit of your name," he tried.

She laughed a mirthless laugh. "Nice try. Look, I just wanted to tell you that I feel we got off to a bad start. First, you dented my car."

"No, I didn't," he said automatically.

"Then you knocked me down."

"No, I didn't."

"And then you caught me in an embarrassing situation."

Now it was his turn to laugh. "You were schlepping a dead body around! You and that toy store guy."

"Like I said," she continued icily, "you caught me in an embarrassing situation."

"And so you decided to kill me and get rid of the body, along with the other sap."

She sighed. "I would like us to start fresh. Forget about the past and move on."

"It's a little hard for me to move on after what you did to me. You tried to kill me, remember?"

"That's not how I remember it at all," she said as she studied her fingernails, which were of the bright red variety, he now saw—same color as her lipstick. He couldn't see her eyes, as they were obscured behind a pair of oversized yet stylish sunglasses, but he knew from their previous meetings they were an icy blue. "As I recall, you saw me assist a shopkeeper in hiding his mistake from the police. Understandable, since they would have thrown the book at him. You can't go around murdering the people who try to rob you, even when they were waving a gun in your face at the time."

"Is that what happened?"

"That's exactly what happened. And if you don't believe me, you can ask your friends at the police station. He was waving that gun and threatening to kill that shopkeeper and the customer who had the misfortune of being in the store at that time, who happened to be me, picking out a present for my niece's birthday. And so when the shopkeeper hit the man over the head, and as a consequence he fell down and died, he asked me not to tell the police but to help him hide the body."

"You should have said no."

"I know. And I still don't know why I didn't. But there you go. And then of course you saw us schlepping that body around, as you so eloquently put it, and I panicked. I have a family to support, you see, and I can't go to prison for some stupid mistake I made."

"If I were you, I'd take my chances," he advised. "Tell the police what you just told me. I think you'll find that Chief Lip is a reasonable guy. He'll understand that you aren't to blame for what happened to that robber. At the most, you're looking at a suspended sentence. Or a fine. Nothing major. Though you definitely made things worse when you locked me up—and the shopkeeper. What were you thinking?"

"I wasn't thinking, all right?" she said irritably. "So can we start over or not?" She held out a finely manicured hand. "My name is Rita Watts—what's yours?"

He wavered. On the one hand, he felt she probably shouldn't be let off so easily. On the other hand, he was a little afraid of this person and wanted this whole thing to be over with as soon as possible so he could go on with his life and didn't have to look over his shoulder anymore. And since the story that Detective Kingsley had told him chimed with what the woman now said, he finally decided that maybe he should give her a second chance.

And so he took the proffered hand and shook it. "Freddie Tottman. Nice to meet you."

She offered him a smile that was more genuine than he had expected.

"Good decision, Freddie. But then you've always struck me as an intelligent young man." She got up. "I'll be seeing you around."

"I hope not," he blurted out.

"Or not," she agreed and walked away.

As she did, he felt himself relax, a great weight lifting off his shoulders. And so he took another bite from his croissant and another sip from his coffee, and felt lighter than he had in days.

He had a feeling that a curse had been lifted and his ordeal was finally over.

CHAPTER 34

When Alec watched Councilwoman Rebekka Lipscombe waltz into his office, for a moment he was speechless. She had always struck him as a force to be reckoned with, and from Charlene's stories, she certainly was a forceful sort of person who knew what she wanted and never failed to get it.

"About my father," she said as she closed the door behind her.

"Yes, I'm sorry about what happened," he said, even though it should be she who was sorry that her father had attacked another man in the rest home and had almost killed him.

"You can't keep him locked up in here, Chief," she said as she leaned on his desk and looked him straight in the eye without flinching.

"N-n-no," he said. "Though it is true that he tried to murder a man last night, Mrs. Lipscombe."

She gave him an indulgent smile. "My father hasn't been himself lately. I think you'll find that the doctors have determined that he suffers from an advanced stage of dementia.

And even though the people at Edith Wale told his family that they had everything under control and that he was welcome there, they still allowed something like this to happen."

"So what do you suggest?"

"I suggest that you let him go, as he's as much the victim here as the other man. I will reach out to Mr. Cooper's family, of course, and offer to compensate them for any inconvenience my father may have caused. And then I'll take him to a different nursing home. One where they're actually able to deal with the very particular issue he's facing."

"Is that a promise?" he asked.

She nodded once. "You have my word."

Frankly speaking, that was good enough for him. He had already been in touch with the prosecutor's department, and they had told him it was an extremely difficult case. Mrs. Lipscombe's father had clearly been suffering from a lessened mental state when he attacked Mr. Cooper, and prison wasn't the right place for a man like that. They, too, preferred if some other solution was found. And if the family was prepared to put him in a more specialized and secure facility, that would save them all a lot of trouble and the taxpayer a lot of money.

"Okay, fine," he said and held up his hand. She shook it with a curt nod.

"I knew you'd see things my way," she said, and straightened. "Charlene never fails to tell us what a great police chief you are, and I happen to agree with her. Thanks, Chief Lip."

"You're very welcome, Councilwoman Lipscombe," he said. And as he escorted her to the officer in charge of their jail cells, he made sure that all the necessary release papers were quickly processed and that the councilwoman walked out with her dad with as little delay as possible.

* * *

"Oh, Dad," Rebekka said with a sigh as they walked out of the police station. "Couldn't you simply behave? Was that so hard?"

Her dad gave her an odd look. "You look familiar," he said. "Have we met?"

She gave him a wry smile. "Yes, we have met a few times."

"I thought so," he said with a nod. "I never forget a face."

"Of course you don't."

A car stood idling at the curb, and when the window was rolled down, Daavid greeted them with a cheerful, "Hey, Dad. I heard you were a bad boy last night?"

"Cut it out, Daavid," she said. "Just take him home with you, will you?"

"Marisa isn't exactly jumping with joy," he said, referring to his wife.

"Well, that can't be helped. Until we find a new place for him, we have to put him up somewhere. I hope you've explained to her she can't leave him out of her sight?"

"She'll be fine," Daavid assured her. "Hop in, Dad. We're going for a drive."

"Do I know you?" asked Dad as he scrutinized his son stoically.

"Ah, don't be like that, old man," said Daavid. "You know we're buds."

"Your face does look familiar," Dad conceded. "And like I just told this nice lady here, I never forget a face. Memory like a steel trap, I have. Never fails."

Daavid grinned, and Rebekka rolled her eyes. "Just get in, will you?"

She opened the door, and their dad got into the car, even though he still seemed hard-pressed to figure out where he knew Daavid from. "Have we met at the golf club?" he asked.

"Yeah, that's right," said Daavid. "We're golf buddies."

"I knew it!" said Dad. "What's your handicap?"

Daavid frowned. "Handicap? I'm not handicapped."

Rebekka slammed the door, and the car drove off. Another problem solved, she thought. Now for the biggest of their concerns: the old Cooper plant and those four imprisoned pensioners. Hopefully, she could rely on Aappo to deal with that part of the business.

"Talk of the devil," she murmured as her phone belted out its ringtone, and she saw that it was her brother. "Shoot," she said the moment she had picked up.

"Ants," he said.

"What are you talking about?" she asked as she put a hand to her perfectly coiffed head and tousled those dark glossy locks of hers that always attracted so much admiration. "What ants?"

"Ants and cats," he specified. "We're being overrun here, Bekka. Place is full of them. Oh, and toddlers, too."

She clasped her teeth together to stop from screaming. Then she counted to ten in her head before she asked, "Please explain to me in simple terms what's going on. Pretend I'm five. Or maybe three."

"Ants and cats and toddlers!" he repeated. "I don't know how much simpler I can put it!"

And then she really did go and scream, causing a passing couple to start violently and give her a wide berth, even while nodding a greeting and muttering, 'Councilwoman.'

Looked like she might have some damage to repair if she wanted to be elected for another term.

CHAPTER 35

Even though Lucian had done us a bad turn, I still felt we shouldn't keep the truth about that kibble from him. After all, he'd been carting so much of the stuff over to his queen by now she must be drowning in it. And all of it laced with that powerful narcotic. Even though initially we may have thought Odelia and Chase and those lab people were exaggerating, I now believed they were telling the truth. Plakka was not a joke, and it just didn't sit well with me that we wouldn't try one more time to dissuade the ant general from feeding the stuff to his colony. And so the four of us set out to give the ant the bad news that the kibble was poisoned and he probably should destroy it. Much to my relief, the weather had slightly shifted, and the day promised not to be such a scorcher as the past few weeks had been. In fact, it was perfectly seasonable weather outside, which only served to improve my good mood.

"Where do you think Gran is, Max?" asked Dooley. Ever since our humans had discovered that Gran hadn't come home last night, he'd been worried about her. But as Uncle Alec had assured us, she probably had spent the night at a friend's place, feeling the hour was late and she didn't want to drive back to her own home but rather crash in her friend's spare bedroom. The fact that she didn't pick up her phone was because she was sleeping late, owing to the fact that she had been up half the night, which the Chief said he had told her many times was not something he could advocate, given her advanced age. But then Gran always did what Gran liked, consequences be damned.

All in all, I didn't think there was anything to be concerned about, and that's what I had told Dooley. To some extent, my words seemed to buck him up, though he wouldn't be fully relaxed until he could clap eyes on Gran and ascertain for himself that she was all right.

Blake's Field stretched out before us, and we made a beeline for the last place we had seen the ants. It wasn't hard to locate the colony, as ant hills have a distinctive conical shape. And as we stood before the structure, I had to say that Lucian and his fellow ant soldiers had done their best. It was a work of art. A nice big heap of sand, and I knew that underneath it, their nest probably stretched out much farther.

"These ant colonies can get huge," Dooley knew. "Underneath our feet are probably thousands of ants crawling right now, or maybe even millions, in tunnels that stretch out in all directions."

We took in the area we were standing in with a look of uncertainty, and I have to say I hoped those millions of ants wouldn't all of a sudden come streaming out and decide that we weren't welcome there.

"Odd that there aren't any of them around," said Brutus.

"Yeah, where are they?" asked Harriet.

It was then that Dooley decided to give the ant hill a gentle nudge with his paw. "Lucian!" he said. "Oh, Lucian! Come out, come out wherever you are!"

"Dooley!" I hissed. "Please don't do that. They'll get upset!"

But even as we waited patiently for the ant leader to come storming out and to ask what we thought we were doing, not a single ant could be seen.

"Maybe they're holding their siesta?" Dooley ventured. "You know, after having worked so very hard, they probably need a break."

"I doubt it," said Brutus. "Don't ants work in shifts?"

"Yes, they're a very organized society," Harriet said.

All of them seemed to know a lot more about ants than I did, but one thing was for sure: after all the activity that had gone down before, it struck me as ominous that the ants would all have disappeared now. And then I got a terrible idea. "You guys, maybe it's that kibble. It's had a deleterious effect on the ants, and now they're all dying down there!"

"Oh, no!" said Dooley. "We should have warned them!"

"We did warn them," I reminded my friend. "But they wouldn't listen."

"That's always the trouble with these powerful leader types," said Brutus, shaking his head. "Headstrong. Think they know better. And see where it got him. Not so fearless now, is he, this Lucian?"

It was then that a tiny ant poked its head out of the ant hill. "Can I help you?" it asked.

"Oh, thank God!" I said. "Are you guys all right down there? Do you need help? A vet, maybe?"

"Now why would we need a vet?" asked the ant with a frown.

"Vets don't treat ants, Max," said Brutus. "At least I don't think they do."

"Probably they're not trained to treat ants," Harriet agreed. "Too small to operate on, I guess."

I could imagine it would definitely be difficult to operate

on an ant, as these creatures might be tough, but they're also tiny.

"Unless you use a magnifying glass," Dooley pointed out. "I'll bet that Vena has a magnifying glass for exactly these contingencies. She's always prepared for anything. Just like a girl scout."

"Okay, so what's going on?" asked the ant. "And why are you still here? Don't you know this is strictly forbidden territory for anyone who's not an ant? And as far as I can tell, you guys aren't ants."

"No, you got that right," I said. "It's just that the kibble Lucian has been taking back to the nest isn't safe for consumption. They laced it with a powerful narcotic, you see, so if your queen has been feeding on the stuff, it might do her more harm than good."

"Unless, of course, ants have such a constitution that drugs don't harm them?" Dooley suggested.

"Our queen is perfectly fine," the ant informed us now. "Thanks for asking."

Call me skeptical, but I still wasn't entirely convinced. "But the kibble—"

"She likes the kibble just fine," said the ant curtly. "In fact, she can't get enough of the stuff. Keeps asking for more."

"Oh, no!" said Dooley. "She's become an addict, just like Max!" He turned to me. "We'll have to ask her to join the Caddicts, Max. Though we can't call it the Caddicts anymore if ants sign up, can we?" He thought for a moment. "They could start a separate group. Call themselves the AAA. Ant Addicts Anonymous."

It seemed like a minor point, and besides, I'd never heard of ants joining a twelve-step program before. It seemed a little far-fetched. "Is Lucian there?" I asked, for I had a feeling we weren't getting anywhere with this ant. When you want something done, always good to talk to the person in charge.

"No, he's gone out foraging," said the ant.

"Foraging?" I asked. "You mean…"

"He's found himself another large batch of that same kibble you just mentioned. And so he's gone there with most of the members of our colony to see if he can't drag it back here."

I knew I was in trouble when the first thought that passed through my mind was a sense of exhilaration that there was more Franklin Cooper kibble in the world and that the ants hadn't yet confiscated it and relegated it to their queen. And so I asked but a single question.

"Where?"

CHAPTER 36

As we passed by the house on our way to this Franklin Cooper Valhalla that the ant had described, we came across Grace. Turns out that the toddler had been looking for us. And not just her, but about a dozen others of her ilk: a dozen little boys and girls who all seemed extremely excited to be enjoying a day out. It took me a while to understand that probably they shouldn't have been there, as infants of their age are supposed to be at the daycare, playing with toys and generally being looked after by the people in charge.

"What... are you doing here?" I asked therefore.

"Well, you wanted us to move that kibble for you, didn't you?" she reminded me. "To bring it from Blake's Field to Grandpa Tex's garden house. And since I can't do it all by myself, I thought I'd ask my friends from the daycare to help me out." She gestured to those friends in question, all of whom were about the same age she was. In other words: far too young to be out and about without adult supervision! "We're ready to rock and roll, Max!"

"But we told you that the kibble isn't there anymore, remember?" I said.

She looked disappointed. But only for a moment. "So where is it?"

"The ants took it," said Dooley. "They took it back to their colony to give to their queen, who's very hungry since she has to keep making new ants to keep that colony growing."

"Okay, so where is this ant colony?" asked Grace. "We'll get them to share that kibble, since it's not fair that they get to keep it all to themselves. And besides, it's cat kibble, not ant kibble."

She had a point, but I had a feeling Lucian wouldn't be impressed by this exercise in semantics.

"You better not go anywhere near that colony," Harriet advised as she nervously watched the other kids inspect Grace's paddling pool. We may not be babysitters, but we still felt a sense of responsibility for the fact that these kids were on our turf. "Ants don't like it when kids go prancing all over their nest. They might turn hostile and attack you. And you don't want to be attacked by ants."

"Oh," said Grace, deflating a little. "So you don't need me to get you that kibble anymore?"

"No, because we have just found out that there's another stash for us to find," said Dooley.

I could have kicked him, but of course I didn't. "Dooley," I said warningly. But it was too late.

"Where?" asked Grace immediately. "We'll help you carry it, won't we, you guys?"

And as one toddler, her little friends all yelled, "Yeaaaaah!!!"

Oh, dear. And since she wouldn't listen to any of my objections, and Odelia wasn't there to stop her, or any of the other adults, we had no other recourse but to allow them to tag along on our trip to the fabled Franklin Cooper factory, where apparently lots and lots more kibble was to be found.

"Just don't eat it," I told Grace warningly. "Because it's not good for you."

"But you eat it, Max," she pointed out. "So it can't be as bad as all that, can it?"

"Well, it is pretty bad," I said. "And I probably shouldn't eat it either."

"Max is an addict," Dooley explained helpfully. "He's trying to stop, but it's not easy. Which is why we all became members of Caddicts."

"What are Caddicts?" asked Grace.

"It's a group of cats that are also addicts," he said.

She thought about this for a moment, then brightened. "I'm also an addict," she confessed. "I'm addicted to candy. Does that mean I'm a candict?"

"Something like that," I said.

We had set out along the road, and I have to say we attracted a lot of attention. Then again, when twelve infants and four cats toddle along the street, they're bound to get a lot of eyeballs. I mean, it's not a sight that you see every day.

It wasn't long before we had left our neighborhood and were en route to the canal zone where most of the industrial activity takes place, so as to keep it removed from the places where people actually live.

A little girl walked next to me and tried to grab my tail. "Why do you have a tail?" she asked, fascinated by the appendage.

"I'm not sure," I said. "Maybe to keep our balance when we're walking on a ledge?"

She couldn't understand me, of course, but still insisted, "Why don't I have a tail?"

"Yeah, why don't we have tails, Max?" Grace insisted. "We love to walk on ledges."

"I sincerely hope you don't," I said, horrified by the notion that she would put herself in danger like that.

"Humans used to have tails," said Dooley, always ready to share the knowledge he has gleaned from watching the Discovery Channel with Gran. "But over time, they didn't need it anymore since they stopped living in trees, and so now all they have is a tailbone where their tails used to be."

Grace felt her tushy for said bone and was relieved to find that it was indeed there. "I want to have a tail," she now announced. "I'll ask Mommy to make me one."

"Yes, do that," I said.

A little boy had been watching Harriet very closely and suddenly burst out, "You're very white!"

"Yes, that I am," said Harriet, who has always been very proud of her snowy fur. "You like it?"

"I hate white!" he shouted. "It reminds me of doctors and hospitals!"

"Bram has been in hospital a lot," Grace revealed. "Something to do with his tonsils."

"I have very big tonsils!" the little boy announced. "The doctor says he's never seen tonsils as big as mine! He says I should probably get a prize for having the biggest tonsils in the world!"

Something told me that having big tonsils wasn't necessarily a good thing, but then of course I'm not a tonsil specialist.

"Why are you so small?" asked another little girl. The question was directed at Brutus, who seemed to take offense.

"I'm not small," he said.

"You're smaller than an elephant," she pointed out.

He couldn't argue with that. "But bigger than a mouse," he riposted.

After Grace had translated his words, she came back with, "But smaller than a house."

"But bigger than a louse!" said Brutus, trying to be funny.

The girl laughed uproariously, and Brutus grinned, happy to entertain.

All in all, it was a fun bunch, and I could see why Grace liked to get other daycare center kids to tag along with her. They were all friends of hers, and she enjoyed spending time with them. I still wasn't fully convinced it was a good idea to be out and about like this, but as long as they didn't get into any trouble, we might get away with it. Also, all I could think about was that fine kibble.

Looked like I was still very much a caddict!

CHAPTER 37

It took us a little while to get to our destination, since neither toddlers nor cats are particularly fast in getting from point A to point B, but since all of us were highly motivated—the cats by the prospect of digging their teeth into that wonderful kibble, and the toddlers by the sense of adventure that even at their age was already prevalent—we arrived at our destination in due course. If anything, all we had to do was follow the ants, since there were so many of them, and all of them traveled at different speeds. We found clumps of them—or battalions or brigades would perhaps be better terms—all along the road, and by following their trail, it wasn't hard to thread our way to the factory which, until not all that long ago, had been a beehive of activity, and whence kibble had been pouring by the truckload—quite literally.

"It's here," said Dooley as he gazed up at the sign over the factory gates that read 'Franklin Cooper Premium Pet Food.' "We found it, you guys. We actually found it!"

"It's beautiful," said Brutus, his voice quivering with emotion. "So beautiful."

"So this is where they made all of that lovely kibble," said Harriet.

"Let's take a look inside," Grace suggested, and without awaiting our response, led her troupe of kids through the gate and onto the factory terrain, ignoring the sign that said 'No trespassing.' Then again, maybe that was merely a suggestion, just like the notion of an expiration date.

Funnily enough, in spite of the fact that the factory was supposed to be defunct, several vans were parked outside the loading bays, which told me that maybe neighbors were using it as a parking lot. And as we went in search of the factory floor, where presumably some of that kibble might still be stored, we followed Grace and her gang of mini-detectives.

"Over here!" the little girl shouted, and waved us over. She had passed through one of the doors that led into the imposing building, possibly the entrance through which over the course of many years, factory workers had entered to start their day shift.

"What a wonderful job that must be," said Brutus. "To make pet kibble all day long. If I were a human, I think I would aspire to do just such a job. Probably the best job in the world."

"Just the smell alone," said Harriet. "To be able to smell that special kibble smell all day long, I can't even imagine how happy those people must have been and how grateful to be working here. Like you said, sugar buns. The best job in the world."

I had a feeling that humans might not agree. Some of them might not like to smell the smell of pet kibble all day long and might prefer to smell the smell of chocolate, to name but one thing, or cookies. But then humans are weird, as we all know, and don't know a good thing when they smell it.

NIC SAINT

"Look at that!" said Grace when we had joined her and her gang of little rascals.

And before us spread a veritable panorama of joy: a mountain of Franklin Cooper kibble, stacked high—all the way to the ceiling.

"You hit the jackpot!" I told the little girl.

"Just following my nose," she said, wiggling said organ happily.

"Odd that these would have been left here," said Brutus. "Wouldn't they have sold the goods, after the factory closed?"

"Maybe they forgot," I said. "Or maybe the factory went bust, and things were left as they were on the day it went belly-up."

We walked into that ginormous storage room, awed to be in the presence of greatness, goodness, and deliciousness, when all of a sudden, we discovered that we weren't alone: crawling all over those bags of kibble were thousands upon thousands of ants.

"Not again!" said Harriet as we watched the ants form one of their fabled conga lines and carry off that kibble. Overseeing their heroic efforts was Lucian.

"This kibble is ours," said Lucian coldly. "We got first dibs."

"You can at least leave some of it for us!" said Brutus.

"No can do," said the ant general. "We have a very large colony, getting bigger every day. Lots and lots of mouths to feed. So please leave, and take those horrible monsters with you."

It took me a moment to realize that he was referring to Grace and her gang, but when I did, a sort of righteous anger grabbed hold of me. "You will not refer to those kids as monsters," I said. "They are absolutely lovely, and if not for them, we wouldn't even have made it all the way here." It was true that Grace had been the driving force behind today's expedition. "And also, you are going to leave some of that kibble to us, Lucian. Cause if you don't…" And as I thought of an appropriate threat that would get the ant leader to play ball, he gave me a sort of mocking look.

"Just give up, Max," he suggested. "You don't have it in you."

"If you don't give us that kibble," I repeated. "We will… we will…"

"You'll do what?" he said.

"We'll destroy your nest!" said Brutus.

"You and whose army?" said the ant chief.

"We'll dump my paddling pool all over your ant hill," said Grace, who had joined the conversation. "And let me tell you that's a lot of water, Mr. Ant!"

"Are you sure you want to do that, Grace?" asked one of her little friends. "You promised we could come and play in your paddling pool, remember?"

"My daddy will fill it up again," she said. "And if necessary, we'll dump that second load on your ant nest also!" she added for Lucian's sake. "And a third. Until you promise to leave some of this kibble for my cats."

"Oh, so these are your cats, are they?" asked Lucian, but I could see that her words had given him pause. He thought for a moment. "Okay, how about a bag each?"

"Ten bags each," I said. "And you're still doing a great deal, as there must be thousands of bags here."

"Max, maybe we shouldn't," Dooley now said, offering the contrarian view. "I mean, we're all trying to get rid of this habit, aren't we? So this isn't going to help."

"Yeah, Max," said Harriet. "Maybe we should take this as a sign."

"Why would you want to kick the habit of eating kibble?" asked Lucian. "I don't understand."

"Because there's something in this kibble that's highly

addictive," I told him. "It's a substance called Plakka, and it's not good for you." We had told him this before, but clearly it hadn't registered.

"Is that so?" he said pensively. "You know, I have noticed that our queen has started behaving a little strangely lately. Ever since she started gobbling up this kibble, in fact. Mood swings, and strange outbursts. Not her usual sunny self, I mean. She even accused me of hogging that kibble and keeping it all for myself, which is a blatant lie, I promise you."

For a moment, we felt we were all at a crossroads. Maybe we should leave the kibble where it was, and not take any of it? I mean, the temptation was extremely powerful, and I felt myself succumb to the appeal of taking one more pellet of that delicious stuff, imbibing it whole and then another, and another...

And as we all pondered this dilemma, suddenly a man came wandering into the storage room. He was a powerfully built man, and I recognized him as one of the men we had seen at the house where that unfortunate baker had been held, and also the toy store owner.

The moment he came upon us, he seemed to have trouble believing his eyes, for he did a double-take, then rubbed his eyes for a moment before taking another look. Then he did an about-face and hurried out of that room, grabbing his phone as he did.

"I have a feeling that we may be in trouble again," I told the others.

"Looks like this kibble is increasingly popular," Harriet added.

"Who was that guy?" asked Lucian.

"He belongs to a gang of drug dealers," I told him. "They've been dealing this kibble on the streets of Hampton Cove, both in the form of pills and also powder."

"Powder?"

"They inhale it," Brutus explained. "And also smoke it."

Lucian shook his head. "Just when you think you've seen it all…"

"I think we better get out of here, Max," Grace said. "That man didn't look very nice. I'm sure he wants to tell Mom and Dad what we've been up to, and if they know we've eloped from the daycare, there will be hell to pay."

I could have told her that there would be hell to pay regardless, for by now the person in charge of that daycare would have discovered that a large portion of their regular customers had escaped, but it seemed more important to come up with a plan of campaign. And so I asked Lucian, "So what do you want to do about this kibble?"

"I'm not sure," the ant general confessed. "On the one hand, it looks like the perfect food for my colony. On the other hand, if what you're saying is true, maybe we shouldn't go anywhere near the stuff."

His words confirmed a thought I'd been harboring: that I probably shouldn't go near the stuff myself. But before we could come to an agreement that we would both leave things as they were, half a dozen men came charging into that room, led by the same goon who had wandered in before.

"I don't believe this," said one of the goons. "Cats and kids!"

"And ants," said one of his colleagues. "Will you look at those ants!"

"They're stealing our merchandise!" said a third goon.

"Put the hose on them!" suggested a fourth.

"And ruin our product? Are you kidding me?" asked number one.

And since they seemed to have a hard time deciding how to proceed, we made full use of this lull in the proceedings to do a runner.

Out the door, we went, and across the factory floor, the

same way we had come. Only when we were passing in the direction of the exit, suddenly a familiar scent entered my nostrils. It smelled very much like… Gran!

CHAPTER 38

Vesta had been pacing the floor of her jail cell incessantly since the sun had cast its rays through the grimy little window located high in the wall. The room had probably been used as a janitor closet back in the day the factory had still been in full operation, but now was empty, bar from the four members of the neighborhood watch. After they had been unceremoniously locked up, she had tried everything to get that metal door open, from banging and screaming to giving it a kick with her foot—something she now regretted, for her foot hadn't stopped hurting ever since. Francis had implored her to calm down, and said the only thing that they could do was pray, and had given the example by offering a prayer to the good Lord himself and hoped that He would make their captors see the light, that making four pensioners sleep on a cold concrete floor was akin to torture, but so far it hadn't done a lot of good.

"Sooner or later, someone will come looking for us," Cliff offered. "Lily said she was going to drop by the apartment later today, and when she can't find us, she will go to the police, I'm sure."

"No, she won't," said Mindy. "I told her just yesterday that we were considering taking a trip to the lake, and so she'll simply conclude that we went and forgot to tell her."

"My parishioners will miss me," said Francis. "Though they might not call the police," he added on a lesser note. "They might pray for my soul, though," he said, cheering up again. "And as we all know, there's power in numbers."

"I'm not sure that also applies to prayer, Francis," said Vesta.

"How about you?" asked Mindy. "Isn't someone going to miss you?"

"Oh, for sure," she said. "My daughter, my son-in-law, my granddaughter, my cats..."

"And don't forget about your son," said Francis. "When Alec hears that you've gone missing, he'll organize a search party for sure, right?"

To be honest, Vesta wasn't so sure that Alec would do anything of the kind. Numerous were the times when she had made a mess of things, and every time, Alec had been forced to shoulder the blame. It wasn't impossible that this time he'd simply ignore his sister's pleas.

"Scarlett will miss me," she said. "We were supposed to meet this morning to have a drink at the Star Hotel, and when I don't show up, she'll know that something went wrong last night."

She now wished that Scarlett was there with them. She liked this new couple, but Scarlett was the one person in the world she could always rely upon to come up with some bright idea. They seemed to bring out the best in each other.

And since kicking against that door or screaming until she was hoarse didn't seem to do them any good, she plopped

PURRFECT KIBBLE

herself down on that cold floor and gave herself up to thought. And it was as she had been thinking hard and coming up with nothing at all, that she thought she heard a soft meowing on the other side of that door. Moments later she was on her feet. "Max, is that you?" she asked, hope filling her heart until it was ready to burst. She should have known that of all the people in the world it would be Max who'd find her!

"What are you doing in here, Gran?" asked Max.

"We're all locked up in here," she said. "Me, Francis, Cliff, and Mindy."

"We'll get you out," the large cat promised.

She didn't know how he would accomplish that amazing feat, since cats aren't known to turn keys in locks and open doors. But moments later it actually happened as he had promised: the key turned in the lock and the door swung open. And much to her surprise, before her stood not only her four cats but also Grace, accompanied by a dozen other kids!

"Oh, you darlings!" she cried as she clasped her great-granddaughter in her arms.

"Let's not dawdle," Francis suggested, and that was actually excellent advice.

And so they all hurried out of there, and in the direction of the exit. And they probably would have made it, if not suddenly a blond-haired woman who looked very familiar blocked their passage.

"Not so fast," said the woman.

"But... aren't you Councilwoman Rebekka Lipscombe?" asked Mindy.

"In a wig!" said Cliff. "You're absolutely right, Mindy. I hadn't recognized her before."

The woman seemed embarrassed to be recognized, and suddenly Vesta realized she must be the one behind this whole thing. Which also told her they'd never get out of there, now that they had seen her.

"Father Reilly," said the woman with a nod to the priest.

"Are we glad to see you, Councilwoman," said Francis. "Some very bad people locked us up in there."

"Francis," said Vesta warningly.

"I can only guess that they're connected to this gang of drug dealers that Vesta's son has told her about," he continued, paying her no mind. "So you're raiding the place, are you?"

"Francis!" said Vesta.

"What?"

"Councilwoman Lipscombe isn't raiding the place. She is part of this drug gang."

The woman grimaced. "You always were too clever for your own good, Mrs. Muffin," said Rebekka Lipscombe. "And far too nosy. With that stupid neighborhood watch of yours."

Francis seemed surprised. "But Rebekka! I baptized your boys!"

"I know."

"I married you and Dirk!"

She sighed heavily. "I promise you this will hurt me more than it hurts you," she said, and took a gun from her pocket and waved it in their faces. "Back in the box, the lot of you." She then glanced down at the four cats and the collection of toddlers. "And that goes for you, too."

Vesta could have told her that it's easier to shepherd a herd of cattle than it is to tell a group of kids to do as they're told, and what happened next bore this out. In spite of the gun being leveled at them, Grace and her friends didn't seem to like that this woman was threatening them, and so as a group, they all rushed forward and gave the woman a vicious kick in the shin. The gun went flying, and the next moment the woman was nursing her injured limb while hopping about on one foot and cursing freely.

More of those goons came running, and as they did, she saw that they were covered with ants, and instead of attacking them, they simply raced right past them, their faces contorted in pain while they desperately tried to get rid of the thousands of ants that crawled all over them and got into their eyes, mouth, and ears.

"They threatened to use the hose on them," Max explained. "And they don't like that."

"They've declared war on the gang," Dooley added. "So things are about to get ugly, Gran."

"Those ants are vicious!" Cliff declared.

That, they certainly were. And since Rebekka appeared to be the ringleader of this whole business, Vesta grabbed her by the lapels and swung her into the room she and her fellow neighborhood watch members had just left, and slammed the door closed on her.

"That should teach her," she said as she locked the door. Then she picked up the phone the woman had dropped and called her son. "Alec! You'll never believe what happened!"

CHAPTER 39

I found myself seated on the porch swing next to my friends, but also next to our new friend Lucian. The ant—small in size but great in courage—looked a little downcast, as he had just discovered that the kibble he had been so efficiently collecting for his queen was no good and had to be removed from the colony as waste. And since I was still suffering from withdrawal symptoms from eating that same kibble, I wasn't exactly feeling on top of the world myself, and the same could be said about my three friends.

"Looks like I'm not going to be meeting any famous celebrities in our Caddicts group," said Harriet sadly. It had taken her a while, but she had finally realized that celebrities may be a lot of things but they're not well-versed in the language we speak, and so they would never join our meetings.

"I keep picturing that mountain of kibble," said Brutus. "And knowing all of it will be destroyed just makes me sad, you know."

After the gang had been arrested and put behind bars, the town council had finally stopped dragging its feet about repurposing the building that used to house the Franklin Cooper operation. The kibble that had been left on the premises was all going to be destroyed, and the machines sold. The building itself was going to be repurposed by a new pet-food-producing company, whose name was still a secret.

The scandal that had erupted after Rebekka Lipscombe had been revealed as being behind a local drug gang had brought turmoil to Town Hall, and even though a lot of people blamed Charlene, and demanded that she relinquish her position and call for new elections, so far she was holding on, and might even survive this crisis. She wasn't the only one who had been fooled by the councilwoman.

"What's going to happen to your queen now, Lucian?" asked Dooley. "Won't she be hungry now that she can't eat that kibble anymore?"

"I'll find something else," Lucian assured us. "It's just that it took us ages to drag all of that stuff into our colony—we had to dig extra tunnels and storage space—and now we have to get it all out of there again and somehow get rid of it."

"Put it back into the police van," I suggested. I'd already confessed to Odelia what we had done, and even though she was angry with us for stealing a police van, she understood that we had been motivated by an urgent and powerful need to safeguard our favorite kibble. She had told her uncle about the van, and one of these days he'd send an officer to pick it up. If by that time Lucian had managed to load it up with the kibble again, they could drive it straight to the landfill where they could dump the lot and be rid of it once and for all.

"Now that Franklin Cooper is finally a thing of the past," said Brutus, "maybe we should resume regular rehearsals of cat choir? I mean, we won't be needing the Caddicts group anymore, will we?"

"Oh, but we will," said Harriet, bridling a little. "There's lots of other stuff cats are addicted to apart from that kibble. Haven't you been listening, snookums? Buster is addicted to chocolate, Tigger to feathers, Misty to tennis balls, Missy to sponges and Clarice to shoes. So I feel it's important to keep these meetings going. And also," she added, "I've just had a bright idea."

"Oh, dear," I murmured.

"Celebrities may not attend our meetings, but guess what celebrities love even more than money and fame? Their pets! All celebrities have pets, and pets have addictions, so they'll flock to our meetings in droves. And where celebrity pets flock, so do their beloved owners. So I can bet you right now that before long we will be trending on social media!"

"I hope not," I said, deciding I couldn't let this pass without a comment.

"Caddict meetings aren't supposed to trend on social media, sugar lips," Brutus chimed in. "They're supposed to be meetings where pets can anonymously reveal to other pets about the problems they face."

"I'm sure the anonymous part is just a suggestion," said Harriet. "Just like expiration dates and 'No Trespassing' signs. Nobody likes to be anonymous. Anonymous is boring!"

"I want to be anonymous," said Grace, who had toddled up to us, clutching a hamburger in her hand. "If I were, people wouldn't be ratting me out to my mom and dad. And I wouldn't be grounded."

We all smiled. She might just be the youngest kid who had ever been grounded. Gran had pleaded with Odelia to let her off the hook, arguing that if Grace hadn't been there, Rebekka Lipscombe's gang would never have been caught, and she and her fellow watch members might still be locked up in that old factory or, worse, be buried underneath it if

Rebekka had her way. But Odelia probably had a point. Grace was far too young to be gallivanting off on her own.

We all watched that hamburger with relish, and finally the girl understood why we were looking at her like that. And so she broke the burger into pieces. "You get a burger," she told me, "and you get a burger, Dooley. And you get a burger, Harriet. And you get a burger, Brutus." She wavered when she saw Lucian rear himself up on his hind legs but finally overcame her natural disinclination to associate with small bugs with mandibles and handed him a tiny piece of burger. "I don't even know if ants like burgers."

"Oh, you can bet we do," said Lucian happily as he munched down on the treat. And then his eyes lit up. "And I'm sure my queen will love it as well." He cocked his head as he directed a quizzical look at me. "You wouldn't happen to have more of this stuff, would you?"

"Don't you guys eat grass or something?" I asked. "Or nettles?"

"We eat everything, Max," said Lucian. "Absolutely everything." He wiggled his antlers. "Though I have to say this stuff is pretty darn tasty. Sign me up for a hundred pounds."

"A hundred pounds!"

"I have a colony to feed, buddy."

It was true that he had been instrumental in catching that nasty drug gang, and so I promised that I'd put in a good word with Odelia about supplying his colony with some prime grub. He certainly had earned it, with all the hard work he'd put into schlepping that kibble from one place to another and then back again.

I suddenly noticed the gleam in Harriet's eye as she regarded the small ant. Then she whispered to Brutus, "Such devotion to his queen, papa bear. Such dedication."

"Yes," said Brutus hesitantly as he shot me a look of panic.

"Must be really something for a queen to experience such a level of, well, not to put too fine a point on it, worship."

"Yes, my sparky star," he said.

"What would you do for your queen, angel muffin?"

"Um…" Again he gave me that look of sheer terror.

"Would you travel miles and miles to feed me? Go to any lengths to support me?"

"Well… yes," he said tentatively.

"Of course Lucian commands an army," she said. "Whereas you are only one cat." She now regarded me and Dooley intently. "Though I guess there's you two—if I can call that an army." She straightened. "Max and Dooley, what would you say if I named Brutus a general in my army and you his loyal soldiers?"

"I would say no," I said immediately.

"I'd say it all depends on the pay," said Dooley, taking the mercenary approach.

She shook her head and tsk-tsked softly. "Wrong answer, Dooley. Ask not what your queen can do for you, but what you can do for your queen. Let's try again. Will you be my soldiers?"

I could see which way the wind was blowing, and so decided that maybe it was time to skedaddle. "Well, I'll be seeing you around," I said and hopped off that swing.

"Max, will you be my soldier!" Harriet demanded.

But I was already moving out of earshot, Dooley right on my heel.

"Max and Dooley, get back here at once! Brutus, tell them to get back here!"

"Well…" said our friend.

"This is insubordination!"

"What's insurmortization, Max?" asked Dooley as we traversed into the next backyard.

"Never mind, Dooley," I said. "Just Harriet being Harriet, as usual."

"Oh, then it's fine," he said, relaxing. "I thought she was going to pay us to find food for her, just like Lucian's queen."

"Lucian's queen doesn't pay him," I pointed out.

"Then why does he do it?"

"Because it's in his genetic makeup, I guess."

"And serving Harriet isn't in our genetic makeup?"

"No, it is not," I said determinedly.

"Thank God for that!" said my friend.

We both laughed heartily. Good thing cats aren't ants, or otherwise we'd have to do Harriet's bidding. Bring her food and cater to her every whim. Treat her like the queen she feels she is. And as we snuck into the rose bushes to have a nice long nap, it wasn't long before Brutus joined us. He may be a loyal mate to Harriet, but there are times when even he has to draw the line, and now was one of those times.

"I'm not an ant," he said with a touch of indignity.

"I know you're not an ant, Brutus," I said.

"I am *not* going to be Harriet's slave!"

"Good for you," I said sleepily.

As I closed my eyes, visions of Franklin Cooper kibble drifted before my mind's eye. Try as I might, I couldn't get rid of them. Which is why I opened my eyes again and said with a sigh, "I dreamt I went to the Franklin Cooper factory again."

"Me too," Brutus lamented.

"And me!" said Dooley.

Then we shared a look. "Will you be my Caddicts buddy, Max?" asked Brutus.

"Only if you will be mine," I told him.

"Can you both be my buddies?" asked Dooley.

And that's how we got to be each other's buddies.

A small voice suddenly piped up next to us. "Can you be my buddies, too?"

It was Harriet, and she seemed to have forgotten already about her idea of us being her soldiers. And so we agreed that we would all be each other's buddies from now on and stand by each other's side through thick and thin, come rain or shine, in good days and bad, and especially when some spiked kibble came across our path and seduced us with its delicious taste, amazing smell, and alluring texture.

In other words: just say no to drivel!

EPILOGUE

I don't think I had ever been in a classroom before, so when the four of us walked in, I wasn't sure what to expect, except that there would be a lot of kids and maybe a schoolteacher, as seems to be common on these occasions. This was certainly borne out when we saw that about two dozen ten-year-olds were seated behind desks that were all facing the front of the class, where a table stood, behind which a teacher sat. Behind her, I could also see a blackboard, and on this blackboard, the message 'Grandparents' Day!' was written in colorful letters.

Along with us, just such a grandparent now entered, looking even more nervous than the rest of us. But then he was scheduled to give some kind of speech, something that wouldn't be expected from us, simple spectators. The grandparent's name was Franklin Cooper, and he was the mastermind behind the best kibble in the world, whose reputation was now marred by the scandal it had become embroiled in. As we were waiting in the corridor before being let into the classroom, I could tell that he had found the attention that we awarded him a little nerve-wracking, but then how often do you meet your hero?

Some people go nuts when they come across George Clooney or Taylor Swift or Michael Jordan, and we experienced the same thrill when we first laid eyes on the man who had created that wonderful kibble. Before long, Odelia told us to behave, and so we tried to curb our enthusiasm.

Next to Mr. Cooper, his son sat, whose name also happened to be Franklin Cooper. He even looked like his father, only younger, of course. And next to Franklin Jr., another person sat. This was Freddie Tottman, the baker we had saved from that old house on Alhola Street, and he was there to meet the Coopers, father and son, to talk about plans to restart the old kibble plant. Turned out he wasn't a baker but a mechanical engineer, and designing and building factories was right up his alley. The council had given their approval, and so soon the engines at the old plant would be churning out pet food once again.

And so as we all took a seat at the back of the class, we watched Mr. Cooper take the stage next to the teacher and address her pupils, amongst whom was his own granddaughter Patsy, who had issued the formal invitation for him to come and talk to her classmates. And so he gave us all a brief presentation of the work of a pet food factory owner, and I have to say we gobbled it all up.

In the middle of his speech, Dooley leaned into me. "When they restart the Franklin Cooper factory, are they going to put drugs in the kibble, Max?"

"I think this time they won't, Dooley," I said. "Putting drugs in pet kibble is against the law."

"So why did they put it in there in the first place?" he asked.

Now that was a valid question, and as I understood, it wasn't the Coopers who were responsible for changing the recipe of their fabled and award-winning pet food. As it now transpired, it had been one of Councilwoman Lipscombe's cousins who had hit upon that idea. He had been working at the plant at the time as chief engineer and figured that if pet food was good, narcotically enhanced pet food was even better and would sell a lot better also, which of course had been the case. It was also the reason why the Banyard gang had moved in after the factory had closed down and had started selling off the remainder of the kibble on the black market, figuring it might net them a nice profit, which it had.

Now that the investigation had been brought into the open, and the FDA had released their final report, the reputation of Franklin Cooper had finally been cleared, and a reconciliation had been effected between Mr. Cooper and the rest of his family, as today's Grandparents' Day proved. A little girl raised her hand, and Mr. Cooper smiled. "Yes, Patsy?"

"I want to work in your factory when I grow up, Grandpa!"

"Well, that's fine," he said, and I could see he was touched by the sentiment. He directed a questioning look at his son, who smiled. Looked like Franklin Cooper was about to become a family firm once more.

"If the new kibble doesn't have that Plakka in it anymore," said Dooley, "does that mean it won't be as tasty as it used to be, Max?"

"I think it will be just as good, but not as addictive," I said. "Which is a good thing."

"I hope it will still have the same great taste," said Brutus.

"And the same yummy texture," said Harriet.

"And the same delicious smell," said Dooley.

I had a feeling the Coopers would make sure of that. And since it wouldn't have that pernicious substance mixed in with the rest of the ingredients, it would be safe for Odelia to buy—with an expiration date far in the future.

"Maybe they could also make ant food from now on," said Dooley. "Otherwise Lucian's queen won't have anything to eat. I mean, it's not just cats and dogs that need to eat. I'll bet there's a huge market out there for ant food."

We all smiled. "There may be a lot of ants out there, Dooley," I said, "but since ants don't have owners, nobody is going to buy them any food. And besides, since ants are omnivores, I'm sure Lucian won't have any trouble feeding his queen."

"Any questions?" asked Mr. Cooper now. He seemed glad that his presentation had gone off without a hitch and looked more relaxed now.

"Mr. Cooper?" asked a little girl. "Where do you get your ideas for new pet food products?"

"Well, since we always had cats and dogs ourselves, I had my target audience right at home with me," he explained. "And if they liked something, I knew that other cats and dogs would probably also like it."

It was then that Harriet got another one of her bright ideas. "You guys!" she said. "Why don't we become kibble testers! That way we can eat all the kibble we like, all the time! And get first dibs on the latest flavors and offerings!"

It wasn't often that I found myself saying this, but I did so now: "Harriet, that's a brilliant idea!"

And so it was. In fact, it was the perfect job for us. But when we told Gran, she seemed less excited than we would have hoped. "You'll get fat," she said in no uncertain terms. "Eating kibble all day, every day, you'll all get as big as whales. So that's a no from me."

"And a no from me," Odelia added her two cents.

"And a no from me, too," said Marge.

Humans. Some of them can't wait for their pets to get a

paying job and move out and stand on their own four paws, and others hate the idea. There's a name for that, and it's called the empty nest syndrome. Looked like our humans suffered from this syndrome to a great degree.

But when I explained this to my friends, Dooley didn't agree. "We're cats, Max. We don't build nests."

"It's just a figure of speech, Dooley," I said. "There's no actual nest-building involved."

"I guess we won't be allowed to work for a living," said Harriet sadly.

"Maybe it's for the best," said Brutus. "I can imagine that clocking in every morning and clocking out every night gets a little old after a while. Not to mention shop talk in the canteen. And gossip at the bar."

"I would love shop talk in the canteen!" said Harriet. "And gossip at the bar!"

Odelia stroked her head. "You already have a job," she whispered.

"We do?" I asked, much surprised.

"You work for me, remember? Pet detective?"

We all grinned. How could we forget? We already had the best job in the world, working for the best boss there was, getting paid in kibble and cuddles. And as far as shop talk and gossip went, we had cat choir. And so we forgot all about becoming kibble tasters. I was sure that after our efforts these past couple of days a lot of Franklin Cooper tasty stuff would be coming our way on a regular basis, as a thank you for being instrumental in clearing Mr. Cooper's name and re-establishing the brand.

But when Mr. Cooper asked for the pupils' attention and asked them to give it up for 'Four very brave kitties!' and consequently led them in an impromptu applause in our honor, I have to admit I was still taken by surprise. Deeply moved, we accepted the applause and the cheers with lumps in our throats.

And when Patsy Cooper got up and handed each of us our own signature Franklin Cooper bowl, with our names written on them, and also a set of small pouches of Franklin Cooper wet food, I was so overcome with emotion that I didn't know what to say. Even Harriet was speechless. Odelia discreetly checked the expiration dates on the pouches, then squeezed their contents into the bowls and we happily dug in. I don't think it's too much to say this was by far our best case ever—and certainly the tastiest one!

THE END

Thanks for reading! If you want to know when a new Nic Saint book comes out, sign up for Nic's mailing list: nicsaint.com/news

EXCERPT FROM PURRFECT WATCH (MAX 83)

Chapter One

Carmelo Hinsley had been walking along the road when he crossed paths with an elephant. As he wasn't expecting to see an elephant in downtown Hampton Cove, for a moment he was surprised and paused to see if he was actually seeing the elephant or perhaps the animal was merely a figment of his imagination. He hadn't been drinking, and the elephant wasn't pink, so chances were that wasn't the case. And as he stared up at the majestic creature, a loud voice suggested he step aside unless he wanted to be stepped on. Since it seemed like good advice, coming from an unsuspected source—a cop—he did as he was asked and hurried out of the way to let the animal pass.

He now noticed that the elephant was part of a larger procession of animals, and behind it, a lion walked, being led by a man only dressed in a G-string and with an exotic-looking headdress that wouldn't have looked out of place in a warmer climate. More animals were on parade, and that's when he understood: the circus was back in town, and to

EXCERPT FROM PURRFECT WATCH (MAX 83)

announce the fact, they had decided to organize a parade through the downtown area of his town. He saw clowns, jugglers, acrobats, and a giraffe and thought it was pretty cool to watch. He'd been enjoying a hamburger in his favorite burger place at the conclusion of a business meeting with one of his company's investors, and this was definitely a nice change of pace. In fact, he couldn't remember having been to the circus since he was a little boy, with his mom and dad and his sister, so this brought back all kinds of long-forgotten memories, all of them pleasant.

"Step aside, sir," the cop told another member of the public who ventured too close to the animals to his liking. "Let the parade pass."

He now wondered how long it had been since the circus had been in town. Quite a long time, he imagined, as circuses weren't as omnipresent as they had been when he was a little boy. Nowadays, there were other forms of entertainment that seemed more popular. Which perhaps was a pity, as there's nothing like a nice circus. He saw that a lot of kids stood gaping at the parade, as probably they had never seen anything like it before. And as he wondered if he shouldn't take his girlfriend to the first show, he thought he felt something near his chest, and when he looked, saw that a man was stealing his wallet!

"Hey!" he said, much dismayed. The man seemed startled that he'd been caught, but instead of giving up his endeavor, doubled down and not only tucked Carmelo's wallet into his own pocket but also grabbed his phone and absconded with it. And all of it under the watchful eye of the constabulary!

"Hey, that man is a thief!" he yelled, pointing to the other man as he made his getaway. "He just took my wallet and my phone!"

And since nobody seemed prepared to do anything about it, he decided to go in pursuit of the brazen fellow himself.

EXCERPT FROM PURRFECT WATCH (MAX 83)

He hated it when people touched his personal stuff and thought to treat it as their own. He had been racing after the fellow for about twenty yards when a woman suddenly stepped right in front of him and gave him a hard shove that sent him flying straight into the approaching path of that big elephant! And as the elephant lifted one tree trunk of a leg preparatory to planting it down right on top of Carmelo, he cried out in dismay. In the very last moment, though, someone yanked him up, and as the elephant put down his foot, right where Carmelo had been, he saw that his savior was the very same woman who had given him that fateful shove in the first place.

"I'm sorry," she said. "Are you all right?"

"What did you go and do that for?" he asked plaintively, referring to the shove, not saving his life.

"I'm sorry," she repeated. "I didn't see you."

A very questionable presentation of the facts, as she had been looking straight at him at the time. But since she had saved his life, he decided not to make too big of a fuss of it. The problem was that this intrusion had given the thief the opportunity to escape with Carmelo's personal possessions, and as he gazed in the direction the man had been running, all he could see was the crowd, standing five rows thick, obscuring the thief from view.

"He's gone," he said, but when he looked back at the woman, he saw that he was speaking to thin air, since she, too, was gone. Which suddenly gave him the idea that maybe she had been the thief's accomplice and seeing as how he had been close to catching the culprit, had decided to step in and waylay him, almost sending him to face certain death by being trampled by an elephant.

And since there wasn't anything he could do, he returned to where he had been watching the parade and reported to that cop what had happened.

EXCERPT FROM PURRFECT WATCH (MAX 83)

"I was robbed," he told the officer of the law. "My wallet and my phone—someone just lifted them off my person."

"Better file a complaint at the station," the man advised.

"Can't I file a complaint with you?" he asked.

"I'm just a traffic warden, sir," said the man, even though he looked like a cop to Carmelo. "Best to head down to the station and file a complaint."

Which is how he found himself seated in front of a very friendly and nice-looking young lady at the police station, explaining to her what had just happened.

"You're not the only one," she told him after he had finished telling his tale. "We already had at least half a dozen reports from people being mugged. Looks like there's a gang of pickpockets active in the downtown area."

She didn't give him a lot of hope that his personal possessions would be returned to him forthwith, but at least it was nice to know that he wasn't alone, and that the police were fully cognizant of the fact that pickpockets were targeting people and were eager to catch the gang.

"You wouldn't happen to have the Find My Phone app installed, would you, sir?" asked the young cop.

"I'm not sure," he said, since he wasn't all that technologically minded. "Um, maybe?"

"Do you have a smartwatch with the Find My Phone function activated?"

He showed the woman his watch, and she smiled. "That's not a smartwatch, sir."

"It's smart enough for me," he said.

"Even if you did have the app installed, they probably removed the SIM card by now and the battery, to make sure they won't be found. Most of the other thefts that we have registered reported that their phone simply disappeared off the grid the moment it was stolen."

"Sounds like they're pretty well-organized," he said.

She sighed. "That, they are," she said. Then a crisp and businesslike look came over her. "Don't worry, Mr. Hinsley. When we find your phone and your wallet, we'll let you know."

Once again, he had the distinct impression that she didn't think there was a big chance of that. But since his phone wasn't an expensive one, and his wallet hadn't contained any cash, all he would have to do was replace his cards.

As he got up and shook her hand, she said, "Don't forget to block your cards, Mr. Hinsley."

"Oh, darn it," he said. "I totally forgot about that."

"Better do it now," she advised.

As he left the station, he wondered if he shouldn't have given the police a description of the woman who had almost been instrumental in causing him to die by elephant, but then decided he had already lost enough time. And so instead he headed straight for the bank to get his cards blocked and new ones issued. Before he could get there, though, four cats passed in front of him, and as he wondered why four cats would be wandering along the sidewalk all by themselves, he figured there was no law against it that he could think of. The biggest of the four, a red bruiser with a thick head who looked vaguely familiar, gave him a curious look, and for a moment he wondered if it was going to say something. Then he shook himself. Of course it wasn't going to say something. Cats don't talk. They're barely intelligent, so what would it say? Got milk?

And so they passed, like ships in the night, he entering the bank and the cats going about their way.

Chapter Two

"That guy was staring at us, Max," said Dooley.

"I know," I said. "Maybe we have met him before?"

EXCERPT FROM PURRFECT WATCH (MAX 83)

"Isn't he the guy who works at the bank?" Brutus suggested.

"I'm pretty sure I've seen him at the pet parlor," Harriet said.

"Isn't he one of the caddies at the golf course?" asked Dooley.

The four of us were walking along the sidewalk, as is our habit of a morning, when this man almost stepped on us. Then again, cats probably shouldn't walk side by side but rather slink along in single file, making sure they don't get in the way. But seeing as we have become accustomed to treating Main Street as our personal catwalk, sometimes this golden rule of cat conduct escapes us.

The man seemed to have recognized us also, judging from the way he stared at us. But the moment passed, and before long we had reached the General Store, where we had arranged to meet our good friend Kingman. Through the proper channels, he had made it known that his human, Wilbur Vickery, who runs the store, had just received a fresh batch of some delicious new type of pet food, and he wanted to give us first dibs on the stuff so we could give Wilbur our much-valued opinion.

"I like this," said Harriet as we sat tasting the new stuff. "I like being a taster."

"I like it when the stuff I get to taste is great," Brutus grunted unhappily. He pushed away his bowl. "This stuff is horrible, though. Yuck."

"I don't like it very much either," said Dooley. He gave Kingman a nervous look. "Do I have to eat everything, Kingman? Or can I stop eating now? Because I really don't like it, you know."

"You can stop eating now, Dooley," said our friend with a laugh. "That's exactly how Wilbur knows it's no good. When I eat everything, he knows it's been approved. When I only

EXCERPT FROM PURRFECT WATCH (MAX 83)

take a sniff and don't touch the stuff, he doesn't stock it. It's our personal arrangement, and so far it's worked well for us."

"And for the store's clientele," I added, since no pet owner likes to buy stuff for their precious darlings that they're not going to like. Then again, tastes differ, of course, and I had to say that I actually liked this new addition to the store's product range. "I like it," I said, therefore. "Can I eat it all, Kingman?"

Kingman rolled his eyes. "Sure, go ahead," he said. "Though this is going to send a mixed message to Wilbur, and if there's anything that man hates, it's mixed messages. It makes him feel terribly insecure."

We all glanced up at our friend's human, who sat shaking with mirth behind his checkout counter while he watched an old episode of the Laurel and Hardy Show. I didn't think there was anything that could make that man feel insecure, especially not mixed messages from his cat. Then again, perhaps he had hidden depths that we weren't aware of.

"Okay, so let's put it to a vote," said Kingman. "All those in favor of stocking the new brand, raise your paws."

One paw went up: mine. Then instantly Dooley also stuck up his paw.

"Dooley, I thought you said you didn't like it?" said Kingman.

"I don't," he said. "But I don't want Max to feel alone."

"Oh, Dooley," Kingman said with a shake of his head. "Okay, so all those *not* in favor of stocking the stuff?" This time four paws went up, Kingman's included.

"Dooley, you can't be both in favor and not in favor," Kingman explained patiently. "It's an either-or proposition. No wiggle room possible."

"Maybe I like it a little bit?" he said, giving me an uncertain look.

I gave him a pat on the back. "You don't have to like it for

EXCERPT FROM PURRFECT WATCH (MAX 83)

my sake, buddy," I said. "Just be honest. Do you like it or not?"

"I don't?" he said hesitantly.

"Great, so we've got our vote," said Kingman. "One in favor and four against. Looks like Wilbur won't be calling that supplier to deliver more of his goods. Now how to convey the message?"

"Just tell Gran," Brutus suggested, gesturing to our human, who now came walking along the road, accompanied by Scarlett. The two ladies were en route to the Star Hotel, where they usually enjoyed a coffee and a chat at this time of the day.

"Gran!" said Kingman. "Can you tell Wilbur that he shouldn't buy more of this stuff? Max is the only one who likes it."

Gran gave him a nod, then entered the store and passed the message on to her friend Wilbur. If Wilbur was surprised that Gran would be conveying messages from her cats, he didn't show it. But then I guess long association with Gran as members of the same neighborhood watch had acquainted him with the notion that Gran's relationship with her cats wasn't the usual kind.

"Thanks," said the shopkeeper. "Oh, before I forget," he said, and handed her a small package.

"What's this?" asked Gran as she turned the package this way and that. "You're not trying to make a pass at me again, are you, Wilbur? You know I like you, but not that way."

Wilbur gave her an amused look. "Me, making a pass at you? I wouldn't dare. No, this is the watch you asked me to get for you. For the swimming thing, remember? Fully waterproof?"

"Oh, right!" she said. "Why, thanks Wilbur. I didn't think it would get here so fast."

EXCERPT FROM PURRFECT WATCH (MAX 83)

"What's this?" asked Scarlett, having joined the shopkeeper and Gran.

"The watch I told you about," said Gran. "The clever watch?"

"Smartwatch," Wilbur corrected her.

"What's so smart about it?" asked Scarlett.

"Oh, this baby can do anything," Wilbur assured her. "In fact, it wouldn't surprise me if it's smarter than most people. It's definitely managed to surprise me a couple of times since I got one."

"Where did you buy it?" asked Scarlett as Gran unwrapped the box and showed her the watch, which didn't look all that smart to me, I have to say. But then of course I'm not exactly a watch expert.

"I got it from a guy I know," said Wilbur. "He works for the company that makes them. It's a prototype. You won't find these in any store for at least the next six months or so."

"Does it come with an instruction manual?" asked Gran as she put it on her wrist.

"Not that I know of," said Wilbur. "Though there is a website. I'll send you the link."

"It's got all this medical information," Gran explained. "Can tell you if you're sick or something. Isn't that right, Wilbur?"

"Absolutely," said Wilbur. "Heart rate, blood pressure, sleep tracker, the works. This watch is your own personal physician." He gave Gran a wink. "Pretty soon you won't need a doctor anymore."

"Tex won't like that," said Scarlett. "He won't like being replaced by a watch."

"Nobody is going to replace Tex," Gran assured her. "And definitely not some silly watch." She eyed the fashion accessory with a satisfied eye. "It looks pretty cute, doesn't it?"

EXCERPT FROM PURRFECT WATCH (MAX 83)

"Do they have it in different colors?" asked Scarlett. "In pink, for instance?"

"Pink!" said Wilbur. "What's wrong with black?"

"Well, black is so... well, black, I guess."

Wilbur shook his head. "A pink watch. Just the idea."

The two women took off, and left us wondering if we shouldn't get our own watches as well. "I mean, it's pretty neat, you have to admit, Max," said Brutus. "A watch that will tell you all about your heart rate, your blood pressure, and who knows what else?"

"I've heard that it can count your steps," said Dooley. "How many steps you take in a day?"

"What's the point of that?" asked Kingman. "Who cares how many steps you take?"

I could have reminded him of the ten-thousand-step craze that was still ravaging parts of humanity, but decided the contentious topic wasn't one I wanted to broach at that moment, so I satisfied myself by saying, "I think a smartwatch has definite advantages, but the point is moot, Brutus. I mean, where would we put that watch?"

"Well, on our paws, of course," said Brutus. "Where else?"

I lifted a paw and wondered how I was ever going to fasten a watch to it, let alone a smartwatch. It didn't seem feasible unless they designed a special model for cats, of course. And since the topic seemed to be closed, we decided to take our leave and head on home.

Chapter Three

Dara Cookland had been waiting for the bus for what seemed like an eternity when finally she thought she saw the vehicle appear in the distance, turning a corner and slowly huffing and puffing its way in her direction. Her boss had ordered her to run an errand in town, but unfortunately was

EXCERPT FROM PURRFECT WATCH (MAX 83)

too cheap to give her the benefit of a car she could use, so she had to make use of public transport to get to and from the house. Working for a famous influencer might sound like the best job in the world, but after having worked for Karen McKirdy for going on three years now, she knew it was anything but. Long hours and the extremely demanding and highly volatile emotional state of Miss McKirdy contributed to the fact that Dara's own nervous state wasn't anything to write home about. If anything, she felt she could probably use a break before she actually broke down. But since the money was good, and she didn't have any other qualifications, she didn't think it was prudent for her to quit.

She held up her arm when the bus approached, making sure to make eye contact with the driver, and as it rolled to a stop right next to her, got on the vehicle. Securing her place at the front of the bus, she sighed with relief. It wouldn't be long now before she was at the house, and would be able to give Karen what she had asked her to pick up at the Hermès flagship store at the mall: the newest and very exclusive 'Karen' edition of the well-known Hermès handbag, of which only a handful were being made.

It was an honor that the well-known French luxury goods company had decided to create a special edition of their handbag, dedicated to Karen, possibly the most successful influencer alive today. The company, headquartered in Paris, France, had the handbag shipped to their local store for Karen to pick up, and Dara hoped her boss would be pleased. It certainly wasn't like anything she'd ever seen before, and since she had started working for Karen she had seen a lot. A lot of extreme wealth, which still came as something of a shock to her, even now. The extravagance, the glitz, the ostentatiousness. The dresses, the shoes, the accessories. And to think that these brands simply gifted everything to Karen, for the privilege of being featured on her socials, beggared

EXCERPT FROM PURRFECT WATCH (MAX 83)

belief. Then again, Karen did have over four hundred million followers on her Insta, so that translated into a lot of exposure for those brands.

She held the bag against her chest, making sure it wouldn't be snatched by some happy-go-lucky bag snatcher. If they snatched this particular handbag they'd think they'd gone and arrived in heaven, for even on eBay it would fetch a pretty penny.

She checked her watch, which was a present from Karen, and of which she was still proud. It was a smartwatch, one of the latest designs, and not a lot of people had one. Karen had several, of course, and had been doling them out like candy.

A man now got on the bus and glanced around, looking for a place to sit. Behind him, a woman also got on. For a moment, Dara feared that the man would sit next to her, but fortunately, he moved to the back of the bus while the woman took the empty seat next to her. She didn't have anything against men, but it was true that most muggers were male, and the last thing she needed was to be mugged right now.

She gave the woman a smile and continued to gaze out of the window at the landscape that zoomed by. They had left Hampton Cove behind and were heading along the coastal road, and then beyond that to the so-called billionaire mile, where a lot of the fancier beachfront properties were located, owned by well-known actors, business moguls, and other wealthy folks, one of whom was Karen McKirdy.

The bus made one more stop, and was just pulling up to her bus stop when all of a sudden the woman next to her made a grab for the handbag Dara was clasping in her hands. Lucky for her, she was prepared for just such a contingency, and as she held on fast to the priceless item, the woman gave it a hard yank, which almost dislocated Dara's shoulder. And since she had opened her throat and was screaming at the

EXCERPT FROM PURRFECT WATCH (MAX 83)

top of her lungs, the wanna-be thief became alarmed and finally let go and hurriedly stepped off the bus!

And as the bus driver came from behind the wheel to see what was going on, she pointed to the mugger who was running from the scene as fast as her legs could carry her, and yelled, "She tried to steal my bag!"

The driver cursed and stepped off the bus, but of course it was too late. Stepping on again, he said, "Don't worry, I've got her on film." And he pointed to a camera that was located at the front of the bus and covered the entire vehicle. "I'll call the police," he announced, but Dara quickly shook her head.

"No need," she said. The last thing she needed was to be waylaid and arrive home late. Karen hated it when her personnel arrived late, and she would hate it even more if Dara got involved with the police somehow.

"What do you mean, 'No need?'" asked the bus driver with a touch of annoyance. "You have to report this, ma'am. This person needs to be caught."

"I was mugged the same way last week," another woman announced. "I never even saw them until it was too late."

"Was it the same person?" asked a third passenger, a man.

"I'm not sure," said the woman. "I didn't get a good look at her."

Dara noticed that the woman was also wearing a smartwatch that looked very similar to the one she was wearing. Which was impossible, of course, since hers was a prototype.

"Look, there's no two ways about it," said the driver, who was a thickset man with an impressive Super Mario mustache. "I'm calling the police, and you're going to give them a full statement."

And since he was so forceful about it, Dara meekly nodded. She might be afraid of Karen's reaction, but this driver scared her even more. He was, after all, an authority figure, and as her mom and dad had always taught her,

EXCERPT FROM PURRFECT WATCH (MAX 83)

authority figures were to be respected and obeyed. And so as the driver called the cops and the other passengers all flocked around to comfort Dara and give their versions of the events, one man stayed out of the fray. He was the last man who had stepped on the bus, directly in front of the woman, and Dara noticed how he didn't join the conversation. Instead, he sat playing with his own smartwatch, then placed his phone to his ear and proceeded to softly speak into the device, occasionally darting a glance in Dara's direction. She reckoned he was probably unhappy at the delay, like she was.

It wasn't long before the police arrived, and as she gave them her version of the events that had transpired, and then the other passengers chimed in to corroborate her story, and also the driver, she hoped Karen wouldn't be too upset. But as the very kind officer explained to her, her employer shouldn't be upset. If anything, she should be very pleased that she had managed to save her handbag from being stolen. And it was as she sat talking to the officer, that she suddenly noticed something.

"My handbag!" she said, looking around. "It's gone! I put it down for a moment and it's gone!"

And as she looked around, she saw that the man who had been fiddling with his watch was also gone.

Chapter Four

Michael Gunt scratched his scalp when he saw that the thirty-four bus, instead of moving right along, was still parked at the side of the road, as it had been for the past twenty minutes. At first, he had wondered if it had broken down or maybe run out of gas, but when he saw the cops join the fray, he knew that something much worse must have gone down. And even though he wasn't the naturally curious

EXCERPT FROM PURRFECT WATCH (MAX 83)

type, he still couldn't resist the urge to take a closer look. And so he jumped down from his tractor, which he had been using to dump manure on his fields, and had a look-see. And so it was that he came upon a pretty touching scene: a young woman of rather large aspect stood blubbering like a little girl, complaining that her handbag had been stolen by some hoodlum. And since Michael knew exactly who this hoodlum was, because he had seen him sprinting away with a bag in his hands, he cleared his throat and decided, much against his nature, to butt in.

"Excuse me," he said, tapping the policewoman on the shoulder. "I'm sorry to interrupt, but I think I saw the guy who stole this lady's handbag."

"You saw the thief?" asked the policewoman, who was very pretty, he thought.

"Yeah, he went that way," he said, pointing in the direction of town.

Immediately the woman put her lips to her phone and said, "We've got a witness who saw the thief, Dolores, heading in the direction of town."

"He was picked up by a car," he added helpfully. "Um, gray model, SUV type of car. Maybe a Toyota, but don't quote me on that."

"Was seen getting into a gray SUV, possibly a Toyota, and driving in the direction of town," she spoke into the device. She gave him a nod of appreciation. "That's very perceptive of you, Mr..."

"Gunt," he said. "Michael Gunt. That's my land over there, so I happened to see everything. I thought it was weird that this guy would be the only one who got off the bus, and in such a hurry, too. But then I figured he was probably tired of waiting for the bus to get going and decided to hitch a ride. The only thing that was strange about that was that he went in a different direction than the bus was going."

EXCERPT FROM PURRFECT WATCH (MAX 83)

"Like I said, very perceptive of you," said the policewoman. And then she gave him a smile, and he noticed how she got two dimples in her cheeks, which was pretty cute, he reckoned.

"You're welcome," he said, and he could feel his cheeks flush a little. "If you need my statement?"

"Yes, please," she said. "Can you talk to my colleague over there? He's taking everyone's statement."

And so he ended up having to tell his story twice, once to the cute cop and once to her more businesslike colleague. "So he stole that lady's handbag, did he? What a crappy thing to do."

"Yeah, not all people are as honest as you, Mr. Gunt," said the cop. "You wouldn't be able to give us a description of the guy, would you?"

"No need, Randal!" the woman police officer yelled. "We've got him on CCTV, remember?"

"Oh, that's right," said the cop.

"I wouldn't be able to describe him to you if I wanted to," Michael admitted. "I was pretty far away, and even though I've got twenty-twenty vision, I couldn't make out his face from that distance."

"No, of course," said the cop. He tapped his notebook with his ballpoint pen. "Well, I guess that's all we need from you, Mr. Gunt. If there's anything else you can think of, don't hesitate to give us a call."

"Will she be all right?" he asked, gesturing to the woman still crying buckets.

"The handbag belonged to her employer," the cop explained. "Cost a fortune apparently."

"Oh, one of *those* handbags, huh?" he said. "Chanel or something?"

"Hermès, I think. A genuine Hermès Karen, apparently."

"What's a Hermès Karen?" he asked, not all that familiar

with high fashion.

"It's a handbag made especially for one person," said the cop. "Woman named Karen, um..." He consulted his notebook. "Karen McKirdy."

"A handbag made for one person?" asked Michael. "I didn't even know that was a thing."

"You and me both, pal," said the cop, who was the jovial kind. "According to my colleague Miss McKirdy is some kind of influencer on social media. The lady over there works for her as a personal assistant, and had just got back from picking up her handbag at the mall. So you can imagine how she feels."

"I guess," he said. "Having your handbag stolen is probably not a lot of fun."

The cop slapped him on the shoulder. "Don't let me keep you, Mr. Gunt."

And so he returned to his tractor and continued spraying his fields. He couldn't help but wonder what that nice policewoman's name could be. And if she would mind if he asked her out one time. Then again, she had probably forgotten about him by now, so he decided to let it drop. As a young single farmer, it wasn't easy to find a woman who'd be interested in sharing his life and home, since he was always busy working, and when he did have some free time, and he managed to find a date, the fact that he was a farmer wasn't exactly a major selling point, and second dates rarely materialized.

As he put the tractor in gear and took the turn, he thought he saw something lying in the ditch that separated his plot of land from the road. If he wasn't mistaken, it very much looked like one of them smartwatches. And as he got down from his tractor to pick it up, he looked around for its possible owner. When he didn't see anyone, he shrugged and put it in his pocket. Might be a good excuse to drop by the

EXCERPT FROM PURRFECT WATCH (MAX 83)

station and talk to the cute cop again. Moments later, he was spraying manure, hoping he hadn't smelled too bad when he was talking to her just now. But since she hadn't made a face, probably he hadn't.

Chapter Five

We had been traveling at a leisurely pace in the direction of our home when we came upon a strange scene. A woman stood gesticulating wildly on the side of the road, a car idling at the curb, and a second woman inside the car sat returning the abuse hurled at her blow by blow. In other words, a common brawl, and since our policy is not to get involved in anything as tacky as a brawl, we quickly crossed the road and made sure to give the twosome a wide berth. Those who didn't follow the same policy were a group of onlookers, who stood eyeing the scene with visible relish. Some even held up their phones, filming every aspect of the sordid exchange.

I had no idea what the argument was about, but as far as I could tell, it may have had something to do with shoes. Or at least that's what I assumed when the woman standing on the sidewalk took off one of her stilettos and proceeded to hammer the roof of the car with it, much to the dismay of the person inside. Suddenly, the driver's side door opened, and a man climbed out. Judging from the look on his face, he was determined to put a stop to this abuse, both of the woman and of his car—though if I were to hazard a guess, he was more upset about his car being the victim of the attack than the passenger, but that could be simple conjecture on my part, of course.

"Why do people like to fight so much, Max?" asked Dooley as we passed by the strange scene.

"No idea, Dooley," I said.

"It's because they have a fighting gene implanted in their

EXCERPT FROM PURRFECT WATCH (MAX 83)

DNA," Brutus claimed. "Most humans have it, and so it's very easy to set them off. One touch on that particular button and they explode."

"What button would this be?" asked Dooley interested. "And where is it located, Brutus?"

"It's not an actual button, Dooley," our friend explained. "It's an imaginary button."

"And what does it do, this button?" Dooley insisted.

"Well, if you touch it, they explode," said Brutus.

He now directed a nervous look at the woman on the sidewalk and the man. "I hope they won't explode," he said. "It's going to make a big mess."

"They're not actually going to explode, Dooley," I assured our friend. "Brutus just means that—"

But before I could finish my sentence, an explosion did actually sound, and as we all ducked for cover in the nearest front yard, I wondered if Brutus hadn't been right all along: maybe humans did have the capacity to explode! But when we glanced from behind the white picket fence, slowly raising our heads above the parapet, we saw that it was the car that had exploded and was now burning freely. The woman who had been inside the car hurried out of it, and the three of them, surrounded by that same troupe of lookie-loos, gazed at the vehicle with astonishment written all over their features.

"Better call the fire department," said one of the people who had taken cover along with the four of us. "And get away from there, you idiots! Dewayne! Get away from that car right now!"

He was probably right. If a car can explode once, it can probably explode multiple times.

"It's one of them electric cars," he explained for our benefit. "Once that battery starts to burn, it'll never stop."

"Is that a fact?" I said, both surprised this man would be

EXCERPT FROM PURRFECT WATCH (MAX 83)

addressing four cats and that a battery-operated car would never stop burning. It seemed like an amazing feat. But then I saw that he hadn't actually been talking to us but to another person, also lying next to us. Both men raised their heads over the fence, as afraid as we were that the car would decide to follow up the first explosion with a second. But when the coast was clear, they emerged from behind the fence. One of them turned out to be the owner of the house where we had found refuge and had been mowing the lawn when disaster struck.

"She's a real pain in the patootie," he now remarked to the other man.

"Who, the car?" asked the guy, confused about this statement.

"No, the woman who was making such a fuss," he said. "Her name is Hilda Innalls and she gets into a fight with anyone all the time. Once she even started a fight with me, if you can believe it."

We all gave him the once-over, and frankly speaking I couldn't believe anyone would pick a fight with the guy, as he looked as big as a house and could probably squash that woman like a bug if he wanted to.

"What was the fight about?" asked the man who was so eager to call the fire department.

"The woman in the car is her sister-in-law Lois," he explained. "And for some reason, Hilda thinks that she cheated on her brother Dewayne with another woman, and so she's been telling Dewayne to leave her. And when Dewayne refused, she blew her top." He shrugged. "Same old story."

The guy finally took out his phone, but since the sound of the fire truck on approach already filled the air, he put it away again. "No need," he explained.

We all watched as the fire truck arrived, and immediately

EXCERPT FROM PURRFECT WATCH (MAX 83)

the firefighters extended a type of sprinkler system underneath the car and water started pouring out of the nozzles, directed at the underbody.

"They can't put out this fire the regular way," the guy explained, "since the battery pack is located along the floor pan of the car. Even then, it can take a while before that fire is out. Nasty things, batteries."

"That's why I still drive a regular car," the muscleman said. "Though I probably should switch to electric, like everyone seems to be doing nowadays."

"Never switch to electric," the other man insisted. "They're all connected, you know."

"Connected?" asked the muscleman. "What do you mean?"

"Everything is connected," the man said. "Didn't you know?"

We gave him a strange look, and so did the muscleman, who took a step back, just to be on the safe side, possibly worried that he would also burst into flame.

"Electric cars, phones, watches, computers—we're all being watched," said the guy mysteriously. "It's a big conspiracy to make sure they know everything about us."

As he said this, he pointed to the sky, and we all looked up, fully expecting someone to stare down at us. When all we saw was a nice cumulus cloud and a flock of geese flying over, I figured that maybe the geese were watching us? Somehow I doubted it, though.

"So you don't have a phone?" asked the muscleman.

"That's right," said the guy. "No phone, no smartwatch, no computer, no internet, and most definitely no electric car. I'm fully analog, that's what I am." He shook his head. "They'll never catch me—no way!"

"Is that a fact?" said the muscleman, who didn't look entirely at ease. Then again, I wasn't feeling entirely at ease

EXCERPT FROM PURRFECT WATCH (MAX 83)

either. Just then, a police car came sweeping down the street, its lights flashing and its siren wailing.

The man took one look at the cop car and said, "I'm outta here, buddy. See you around."

"See you," said the neighbor, and we all watched the strange man hurry off as fast as his legs could carry him, but not before darting an anxious look over his shoulder at the officers stepping out of that police car.

Ruminating on the man's words, the muscular neighbor glanced down at a smartwatch lying on his lawn. It looked a little the worse for wear. Almost as if he had driven over it with his lawnmower. He rubbed his wrist, which was red and swollen, and I got the impression he had yanked off the watch and fed it to the lawnmower for some reason. Possibly he hadn't been entirely satisfied with his purchase.

"Why is that man so afraid of the police, Max?" asked Dooley, looking after the strange man.

"No idea, Dooley," I said. "Maybe he doesn't like cops? Some people are like that, you know."

"He's a conspiracy nut," Brutus explained. "And conspiracy nuts see conspiracies everywhere they look. He probably thinks the police are part of the conspiracy, along with watchmakers, electric car merchants, computer companies and mobile phone manufacturers."

"He didn't strike me as fully compos mentis," Harriet said.

I saw that the muscular man was leaning on his fence, eagerly watching the firefighters try to douse that burning car. And since cats are essentially curious animals, we decided to stick around and do the same thing. We may not like to get embroiled in an argument between a couple of brawling humans, but what we do like is a nice spectacle progressing on our block. And since none of us had ever seen an electric car bursting into flames before, we wanted to catch it all so we could tell Odelia about it later on.

ABOUT NIC

Nic has a background in political science and before being struck by the writing bug worked odd jobs around the world (including but not limited to massage therapist in Mexico, gardener in Italy, restaurant manager in India, and Berlitz teacher in Belgium).

When he's not writing he enjoys curling up with a good (comic) book, watching British crime dramas, French comedies or Nancy Meyers movies, sampling pastry (apple cake!), pasta and chocolate (preferably the dark variety), twisting himself into a pretzel doing morning yoga, going for a brisk walk, and spoiling his feline assistants Lily and Ricky.

He lives with his wife (and aforementioned cats) in a small village smack dab in the middle of absolutely nowhere and is probably writing his next 'Mysteries of Max' book right now.

www.nicsaint.com

Printed in Great Britain
by Amazon